Carmen pulled away from him, resisting the urge to rub the place on her arm where he had touched her, where she imagined she could still feel the heat of his hand.

"You can insist all you want, but I'm not going to help you."

"One thing I learned reading Metwater's writings is that he hates cops," he said. "What do you think he'll do if I tell the cult leader he's got one living with him, lying about who she is and spying on him?"

"I could have you arrested for interfering with an investigation," she said.

"You could. But you'd have to deal with Metwater first." He removed his sunglasses and she found herself held by the intensity of his sapphire-blue eyes. His voice was a low, sexy rumble she was sure was intentional. "I'm thinking maybe you would prefer to deal with me."

D1627216

SOLDIER'S PROMISE

CINDI MYERS

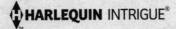

For Morgan and Erik

ISBN-13: 978-1-335-52614-4

Soldier's Promise

Copyright © 2017 by Cynthia Myers

Recycling programs for this product may not exist in your area.

Printed in U.S.A.

HARLEQUIN®
www.Harlequin.com

Cindi Myers is the author of more than fifty novels. When she's not crafting new romance plots, she enjoys skiing, gardening, cooking, crafting and daydreaming. A lover of small-town life, she lives with her husband and two spoiled dogs in the Colorado mountains.

Books by Cindi Myers

Harlequin Intrigue

The Ranger Brigade: Family Secrets

Murder in Black Canyon
Undercover Husband
Manhunt on Mystic Mesa
Soldier's Promise

The Men of Search Team Seven

Colorado Crime Scene
Lawman on the Hunt
Christmas Kidnapping
PhD Protector

The Ranger Brigade

The Guardian
Lawman Protection
Colorado Bodyguard
Black Canyon Conspiracy

Rocky Mountain Revenge
Rocky Mountain Rescue

Visit the Author Profile page at Harlequin.com.

CAST OF CHARACTERS

Jake Lohmiller—This army veteran grew up rough on the streets of Houston and will do whatever it takes to look after his ailing mom and little sister. He's slow to reveal his secrets but fiercely loyal to those he cares about.

Carmen Redhorse—The only female member of the Ranger Brigade grew up in a proud Ute family who had high expectations for their beauty-queen daughter. Her parents want her to return to the reservation to work for the Tribal Police and to marry the police chief, but Carmen wants to prove herself on her own.

Phoenix—Jake's mother has taken a new name and put her past behind her as a member of Daniel Metwater's Family. She hides her poor health out of fear that her hard-won happiness will be taken from her.

Sophie—Jake's little sister is thrilled to see her brother again but worried about what the future holds for her and her mother.

Daniel Metwater—The self-appointed Prophet is used to being in charge, but murder has taken one of his followers and he fears the murderer will come for him next. Is his fear related to his brother's death at the hand of the Russian Mafia, or has Daniel double-crossed the wrong person?

Werner Altbusser—Head of an international smuggling group that sells rare cacti to collectors willing to pay thousands of dollars for a single specimen, Werner comes across as an innocent tourist, but the business partner he cheated has other ideas about the direction the business should go and what will become of Werner and everyone who works with him.

Karol Petrovsky—Werner's former business partner never got what he felt was a fair share of the money from the cacti smuggling. He intends to take over and will deal harshly with anyone who stands in his way.

Starfall—No one is sure why this young woman is following Daniel Metwater, since she doesn't seem to adore him the way his other female disciples do. Starfall has her own agenda and is always on the lookout for a way to make money, whether it's collecting cacti for a smuggler or blackmailing the Prophet himself. But her grasping ways may have gotten her in over her head this time.

Chapter One

Jake Lohmiller raised the binoculars to his eyes and studied the group of women who moved along the rim of the canyon. Wind sent their colorful cotton skirts fluttering, so that they reminded Jake of butterflies, flitting among the wild roses that perfumed the air. The women were gathering rose hips and wild raspberries, the murmur of their voices drifting to him on the wind, their words indistinct.

He shifted his elbow to dislodge a pebble that was digging into his flesh and trained the glasses on a dark-haired woman. Her long, straight black hair, high cheekbones and bronzed skin set her apart from the mostly fair-skinned redheads, blondes and brunettes around her. She seemed out of place, not just because of her appearance, but because of the way she carried herself. She moved slightly behind the other women, her movements both deliberate and graceful, her bearing wary. Jake sensed a tension in her, like a cat poised to spring.

She stopped at the corner post of a falling-down

fence that ran alongside the path the women were following, and turned to stare across the high desert landscape of rock, cactus and stunted trees, one hand raised to shield her eyes from the sun's glare. Jake ducked down behind the rock outcropping he had chosen as his vantage point, though he knew she couldn't see him. Not at this distance. Not when he had been so well-trained to not give away his position.

He had been in the Curecanti National Recreation Area in southwest Colorado for three days, watching the women, learning their routines and habits, and planning his next move. The dark-haired woman turned away and hurried to catch up with the others, and Jake shifted his attention to the oldest woman in the group—a slight, very fair blonde with almost-white hair and light blue eyes. She went by the name Phoenix these days, the latest in a string of names and nicknames she had gone by over the years. He tried to read her mood, to guess what she was thinking or feeling, but at this distance he could tell nothing except that she looked fairly healthy—something that hadn't been the case the last time he had seen her. He clenched his jaw, struggling against the mixture of love and anger that warred in him whenever he thought about her.

He shifted again, focusing this time on the youngest member of the group, and his jaw relaxed. Sophie was growing up to be a pretty young woman, her long brown hair plaited in a single braid that hung to her shoulder blades. She laughed at something one of the others said, and Jake's heart clenched, aching at the sound. The last time he had seen her, she had been ten and crying. Four years had changed her in so many ways, but it cheered him to see her looking so happy, especially since he hadn't expected it—not here.

The women moved on until they were out of the visual field of his binoculars. The silence of the wilderness closed in around him, with only the rattle of the wind in dry tree branches reminding him that he hadn't suddenly gone deaf. He put away the binoculars, then stretched out on his back, the shadow of the boulder keeping the sun off his face. He ignored the hardness of the dry ground and focused on reviewing all the information he had gathered so far. It was time to complete his mission. He had to make contact with Phoenix and Sophie and persuade them to leave with him. But he had to do it without raising alarm. And preferably without attracting any attention from the local cops.

A shadow fell across his torso, and the crunch of a leather sole on gravel had him lurching to his feet, reaching for the weapon at his side. "Keep your hands where I can see them!" a woman's voice commanded.

He held his hands out from his sides and stared at the dark-haired woman. Obviously, she had left the group and circled around, but how had she managed to sneak up on him? Had he gotten so rusty in the months since he had left his unit in Afghanistan? He must have, because, in all the time he had been watching her, he had never noticed the handgun she was aiming at him now.

Carmen Redhorse kept her weapon trained on the man who stood opposite her, thankful that he was cooperating with her orders. He was a big, powerful-looking man, young and strong, and he seemed at home here in this rugged environment. He held his hands at his sides, and his gaze remained focused on her, his manner calm, though it struck her as the calm of a predator who doesn't feel a threat from a weaker opponent rather than that of a man who has nothing to worry about. "Who are you, and what are you doing out here, spying on us?" she asked.

"Who are you, and why should I answer your question?" His expression and the tone of his voice betrayed nothing. She judged he was about six feet tall, lean and muscular. His erect posture, close-cropped hair and deep tan pegged him as a military man—either still on active duty or only recently discharged. An officer, she guessed—he had the air of a man who was used to being in charge.

"I'm the woman who has a gun trained on you," she said. "Trust me, I know how to use it." Until she knew more about him and what he was up to, she wasn't going to let him distract her. "I need you to very slowly remove your weapon from the holster and place it on the ground in front of you."

He hesitated, then did as she asked, his attention focused on her, though she couldn't see his eyes clearly behind the dark aviator sunglasses he wore. He straightened, some of the stiffness gone out of his posture. "What is a cop doing way out here?" he asked.

"What makes you think I'm a cop?" she asked.

"I'm right, aren't I? Everything from your choice of weapon to the way you handle it—not to mention the way you bark out commands—says law enforcement. And not a rookie, either." He shifted his weight, still keeping his hands in view. "So what are you doing in Daniel Metwater's cult?"

His word choice—*cult* instead of *group* or, as Metwater preferred, *Family*—told her he wasn't a fan of the trust-fund millionaire turned itinerant preacher, who was camped with his followers on public land. The women she had been foraging with were part of Metwater's faithful. "What I'm doing here isn't your concern," she said. "And you haven't answered my question—what are you up to? And I'll need to see some ID."

"My wallet is in my back pocket," he said.

"Take it out slowly, and hand it over."

He did as she asked. She studied the Texas driver's license. "Jacob Lohmiller," she read. Twenty-seven years old, with an address in Houston. She glanced across at the Veteran ID. Army—so she had been right about that. And he had been discharged only four months before. "You're a long way from home, Mr. Lohmiller."

"Are you conducting some kind of undercover operation with Metwater's bunch?" Lohmiller asked, accepting his wallet from her and returning it to his pocket. "Are they involved in something criminal?"

The Ranger Brigade—a multidisciplinary task force charged with law enforcement on Colorado's public lands—had suspected Daniel Metwater's involvement in more than one crime, but so far they had found little evidence to support their suspicions. Carmen was ostensibly with the group now, posing as a new convert in order to verify that the group's women and children were not subject to any kind of abuse. She had lobbied hard to take a closer look at the group after a young woman who had been associated with them had died. Her commander had agreed to give her a week, all the time he could spare from the Rangers' other duties. Four days of that week had passed, and Carmen was just beginning to win the other Family members' trust. She couldn't afford to have Lohmiller blow her cover.

"What are you doing here?" she asked again. "Why were you watching us just now?"

"As you said, this is public land. Maybe I came out here for a hike."

She glanced at the pack that lay in the shade of the boulder he had been stretched out beside. "So you were hiking, and you saw a group of women and decided to take a closer look."

He shrugged. "Maybe."

"How long have you been in the area?" she asked. "Where are you staying? Do you have a vehicle, and where is it parked?"

"Why all the questions?" he asked.

"A man focused on a group of women, a man who refuses to account for himself, makes me suspicious. I wonder what I would learn if I brought you in for questioning."

"I flew in to Montrose four days ago," he said. "I've been hiking and camping out here ever since. I have a truck parked at my campsite not far from here."

She nodded. "So, again—why were you watching us?"

"How did you know I was watching you?" he asked.

"I had that sensation of being watched," she said. "I saw a bird startle from your hiding place and decided to take a closer look."

He looked away and mumbled what might have been a curse word. She waited, the gun pointing toward the ground now, but still in her hand.

"I came here to check on a couple of Metwater's followers," he said. "To make sure they're all right."

"Which members?" she asked.

"A woman who calls herself Phoenix and a girl, Sophie. I don't think she's taken one of their loopy nicknames yet."

"You know Phoenix and Sophie?" She knew of

a couple of families who had sent private detectives to check up on their loved ones at the camp, but the forty-something blonde and her fourteen-year-old daughter had never mentioned any other family to Carmen.

Lohmiller squared his shoulders. "Phoenix—her real name is Anna—is my mom. Sophie is my half sister."

It was Carmen's turn to be surprised. "Phoenix is your mother?" The woman looked scarcely old enough to have a son Lohmiller's age, and he didn't resemble her at all.

"She had me when she was sixteen."

"There's nothing to prevent you from walking into camp and visiting your mother and sister," Carmen said. "Why skulk around in the wilderness?"

"I needed to assess her situation, determine the lay of the land and formulate a plan for getting them away from here."

Again, his choice of words was telling. He spoke like a man on a mission. "What exactly did you do in the service, Mr. Lohmiller?" she asked.

"Army Rangers."

She might have guessed. "Your mother is an adult, free to make her own decisions and, by extension, decisions for her daughter," she said. "I'll admit, a wilderness camp with no running water or other facilities is not my first choice for a place to live, but it's her choice. Neither she nor Sophie are in any danger that I've been able to determine. Or are you aware of something I'm not? Some circumstance you believe puts them in danger?"

"No particular circumstance, no. But my mother doesn't have a history of making wise choices."

"*Wise* and *dangerous* are two different things."

"As you said, my mother is free to make her own decisions, but my sister is not. And the so-called wilderness paradise Daniel Metwater likes to brag about is no place for her."

Carmen thumbed the safety on her weapon and shoved it into the waistband of her skirt. Later, she'd replace it in the holster strapped to her thigh beneath the long, loose skirt. For all his obvious agitation and coiled energy, she didn't sense that Jake Lohmiller was any threat to her. "I've talked to Sophie, and she's not unhappy. She's being homeschooled, she's healthy, and she seems to have a great relationship with her mother." So far, nothing Carmen had learned in her time with the Family had pointed to any abuse or neglect, though she couldn't shake the feeling that life in the camp wasn't as rosy as Metwater and his followers liked to paint. The truth was, a week probably wasn't long enough to get a real picture for what was going on. She didn't look forward to returning to her commander with nothing to show for her efforts.

Lohmiller scowled. "What about that creep, Metwater?"

"What about him?"

"I've checked him out. I've read his blog and

newspaper articles about him—everything I could find online. And I've been watching him for a few days now. He collects beautiful women the way some men collect cars. How long before he starts eyeing Sophie?"

His words sent a shiver through Carmen. "I'm sure your mother would never let anything happen to Sophie."

"You don't know my mother like I do."

"When was the last time you spoke to her?"

"Four years ago. Sophie was ten."

"People can change a lot in four years."

"My mom is still making poor decisions. Bringing Sophie out here proves it."

Carmen couldn't argue with that. Though Sophie seemed content enough, following an itinerant preacher didn't seem the best way to bring up a child. But before she could think of a reply, Lohmiller said, "You don't strike me as the typical Daniel Metwater follower."

Knowing that he had been spying on her long enough to feel qualified to make such an assessment annoyed her. "Who do you see as his typical follower?" she asked.

"Disconnected, discontented, idealistic. Young, white and, as far as I can tell, mostly well-off and well-educated. I'm not questioning your education, but the people who flock to someone like Metwater are searching for some idealistic world that he's promising them."

Okay, so he had done his homework. But she

couldn't resist goading him. "You don't think I'm those things?"

"You have a job and a purpose. I doubt if most cops stay idealistic for long, even if they start that way. You seem too down-to-earth and practical to fall for all his mumbo jumbo."

"And I'm not white."

She ignored the pleasant tremor that swept through her as his gaze assessed her. "That, too. Are you Native American?"

"You got it in one."

"So, if you're not one of his followers, that means you're here as a cop. Possibly undercover. What are you investigating?"

Time to get her head back on the job. "I'm not going to discuss my purpose here with you."

"Fine. You don't have to. You can at least give me your name—or whatever name you're going by out here."

Fair enough. "My name is Carmen. Carmen Redhorse."

"Well, Officer Redhorse, the fact that you're here means something is going on in camp that has the cops suspicious. And that means my sister and my mother don't belong there."

"Then you need to talk to your mother and stop lurking in the wilderness," she said. "Some people might get the wrong idea."

"You're the only person who knows I'm here. I

can't control whether your ideas about me are wrong or not."

Had he meant the comment to sound vaguely sexual? Was he trying to provoke her, or was it just his nature? She glanced toward the canyon rim. The other women were long out of sight now. She had told them she wanted to walk back alone, to think about some things, and had promised to catch up with them later. But how long could she stay away before someone came looking for her? "Are you going to talk to your mom?" she asked Lohmiller.

"I'll talk to her," he said. "And what do you think she'll tell me?"

"I have no idea."

"Yes, you do. You've been hanging out with her for at least three days. You must have made some judgments about her. So, tell me what you think she'll say when I ask her to leave Metwater's little cult and come live with me?"

"She'll tell you she and Sophie are happy here, that Daniel Metwater changed her life and she doesn't want to go with you."

He nodded. "Exactly. So talking to her isn't going to be enough. I have to find a way to convince her to leave—with Sophie."

"That's between you and your mother. I can't help you." She started to turn away, but his hand on her arm stopped her.

"I think you can help me," he said. "In fact, I insist."

She pulled away from him, resisting the urge to

rub the place on her arm where he had touched her, where she imagined she could still feel the heat of his touch. She might have known he was the type who thought he could boss her around. "You can insist all you want, but I'm not going to help you."

"One thing I learned reading Metwater's writings is that he hates cops," he said. "What do you think he'll do if I tell him he's got one living with him, lying about who she is and spying on him?"

Metwater would be furious if he learned she was a cop, but that didn't mean he would do anything more than kick her out of his camp. But even though she didn't have any proof that he was involved in anything illegal, everything she knew about him told her he was capable of violence. Still, she was a cop. She knew how to look after herself. "I could have you arrested for interfering with an investigation," she said.

"You could. But you'd have to deal with Metwater first." He removed his sunglasses, and she found herself held by the intensity of his sapphire-blue eyes. His voice was a low, sexy rumble she was sure was intentional. "I'm thinking maybe you would prefer to deal with me."

Chapter Two

Jake knew his words had gotten through the tough attitude she wore like a shield. A rosy flush burnished Officer Redhorse's cheeks, and he could almost see the sparks of anger in her eyes at what he could admit was his clumsily delivered threat. He wasn't sure if she would scream at him or go ahead and shoot him, so he hastened to try to repair the damage.

"Look, all I'm asking is for you to help me out a little," he said.

"I can't help you," she said.

"You can talk to my mother. Tell her you think it's a good idea for her and Șophie to come with me."

"I hardly know your mother," she said. "Why would she listen to me? And I know even less about you. I have no way of knowing if going with you is a good idea or not."

Couldn't she see that he was a good guy? Well, maybe not. "Check me out," he said. "You'll see I don't even have a traffic ticket."

"Just because you've never broken a law doesn't

make you a good guy. Daniel Metwater doesn't have any traffic tickets, either."

He winced. Then another idea occurred to him. "Does Metwater trust you?" he asked.

She looked as if she had tasted something sour. "I'm not sure *trust* is the right word."

"But he likes you," Jake said. "He's attracted to you. You're a beautiful woman, and you're a novelty."

"Because I'm not his usual white and desperate type?"

Because that tough, don't-touch-me attitude of yours is sexy as all get-out. But he thought better of saying that. He was already in enough trouble here. "From what I've seen and heard, the Prophet likes pretty much all young, attractive women—at least, the ones who follow him around and hang on his every word. If you're working undercover in his camp, I assume you're playing the part of devoted disciple."

She pressed her lips together but didn't comment.

"Maybe I can help you out," he said.

"I don't need your help."

"I might be able to find out things you can't. I could talk to the men in camp, let you know what I hear."

She shook her head. "Talk to your mother, but leave me out of it." She turned and walked away.

He watched her leave, her back straight and her confident stride quickly lengthening the distance between them. Should he follow her? He was going to have to go to Metwater's camp sooner or later to confront his mother. He would have liked to have had the pretty cop on his side. The meeting with Phoenix wasn't going to be an easy one, and it would have been good to have an ally. But, if he had to, he'd do the job alone. He was used to working solo—he'd been on his own since he was a teenager. And he knew how to tackle tough jobs. He had already let his sister down once. He wouldn't let that happen again.

He waited a moment to let Carmen get ahead of him, then started to follow. He would see what she did when she got to camp, then make his decision about when to approach his mother.

Before they reached camp, however, Carmen caught up with the other women. He was too far away to hear what was said, but it appeared that a couple of the women greeted her. Then a figure broke from the group and ran up to Carmen. Though Jake couldn't hear what the girl was saying, he recognized Sophie, and she was clearly agitated. Carmen put a hand on the girl's shoulder, listening, then she and Sophie turned and headed back toward Jake.

He walked out to meet them. Sophie stared at him, eyes wide. "Jake? Is that really you?"

"It's me, sis." He held out his arms, and she ran to him and buried her head against his shoulder. The feel of her—bigger than the last time he had seen her, but still so slight and vulnerable—sent a tremor through him. He loved her so much. Why had he stayed away so long?

"Thank God you're here," she said.

He pulled her away a little, so that he could see her face. "What's wrong?" he asked. "Why are you so upset?"

"It's Mama. Something's really wrong with her." She grabbed his hand and started leading him forward. "We have to hurry, before it's too late."

CARMEN FOLLOWED BEHIND Jake and his sister. If she had had any doubts about telling Sophie of her brother's arrival, she knew now she had made the right decision. Sophie walked with one arm wrapped around Jake's waist and looked up at him as if she couldn't believe he was here. For his part, Jake studied his sister as if he couldn't get enough of looking at her.

"Tell me exactly what happened," he said as they headed toward Metwater's camp at the foot of Mystic Mesa.

"We were walking back to camp, and Mama just collapsed," Sophie said. "I mean, one minute she was fine, and the next she just—fell over." The girl looked back at Carmen. "Starfall and Sarah got a couple of the men to carry her to the Prophet. They said he would know what to do for her."

"Has Phoenix complained of feeling bad lately?" Carmen asked.

"No. She's just acted, you know, normal." Sophie turned back to Jake. "I still can't believe you're here. What are you doing?"

"I came to see you." He tried to smile, but the

expression didn't reach his eyes. "You're growing up fast."

Sophie hugged him tighter. "I've missed you so much."

"I've missed you, too." His eyes met Carmen's over Sophie's shoulder, as if challenging her to deny that his sister loved him and was glad to see him.

"Mom's going to be so happy to see you, too," Sophie said.

"Is she? She wasn't very happy with me last time we spoke."

"She was just worried about you joining the military. But she's in a different place now. A better place." Sophie frowned. "Or she was, until this."

"Maybe the heat got to her," Carmen said. "I'm sure she'll be fine." She touched Jake's arm. "You need to hide your gun before we get to camp. Walking in with it visible like that will only cause trouble." She had already tucked hers back into the holster on her thigh.

She expected him to argue, but he nodded. "Okay." He unstrapped the holster from around his waist and stuffed it into his pack. Sophie watched, wide-eyed and silent.

The US Forest Service allowed dispersed camping for up to two weeks outside of designated campgrounds. Through mysterious political connections, Daniel Metwater had wrangled a permit for his group to settle for an extended period in this remote area, near a natural spring at the base of a rocky mesa in the high desert landscape of Curecanti National Recreation Area. This was the third such camp the group had occupied in as many months. Like the others, it consisted of a motley collection of trucks, campers, tents and makeshift shelters, grouped in a rough oval around a central campfire.

A large, late-model motor home was parked at one end of the oval, solar panels winking from the roof. "That's where the Prophet lives," Sophie whispered to Jake.

"Starfall." Carmen called to a woman with dark, curly hair who was wiping the face of a naked toddler outside a large, white tent. "Where is Phoenix?"

"She's with the Prophet," the woman said. She stared openly at Jake. "Who is he?"

"This is my big brother, Jake," Sophie said. "He wants to see Mom. Is she okay?"

"She'll be fine," Starfall said. "She's resting now and shouldn't be disturbed."

"Is your Prophet a doctor?" Jake asked.

Though Starfall was at least a foot shorter than Jake, she managed to look down her nose at him. "He is a spiritual healer."

Jake started toward the motor home, but Sophie held him back. "We're not supposed to go into the Prophet's home without an invitation," she said.

"I'm not one of his followers," Jake said. "I don't have to play by his rules." He gently uncurled her fingers from around his arm and started for the motor home again, Carmen close behind him.

Sophie caught up with them as they climbed the steps to the RV. Jake pounded on the door.

He had raised his fist to knock again when the door eased open, and a pale blonde peered out. Andi Mattheson—who now went by the single moniker Asteria—was one of the reasons Carmen had joined Metwater's Family. The daughter of a former US senator was eight months pregnant and, as far as Carmen could determine, hadn't seen a doctor in months. So many of the Prophet's followers were young women who were either pregnant or mothers to small children that Carmen wanted to determine if they were receiving the necessary care. Andi frowned at the tall, imposing man leaning over her, then looked past him to Carmen. "What do you want?" she asked.

"We're here to see Phoenix," Jake said.

"This is Phoenix's son, Jake Lohmiller." Carmen stepped up beside him. "Sophie told us her mother had fainted and, naturally, he's concerned."

"She's fine," Andi said. "She just needs to rest." She started to close the door, but Jake flattened his hand against it, holding it open.

"I want to see her," he said.

"The Prophet—" Andi began.

Jake didn't let her finish. He shoved past her into the motor home. Carmen and Sophie followed. "Phoenix?" he called.

"Mama?" Sophie echoed.

Daniel Metwater, dressed in his usual outfit of loose, white shirt and trousers, his dark, curly hair framing the intensely handsome face of a male model, appeared in the doorway that led to the back of the RV. "What is the meaning of this disturbance?" he asked.

"I'm here to see Phoenix." Jake started to move past Metwater, but the Prophet blocked him.

"Phoenix is resting," he said.

"I'm going to see her anyway." He took Metwater by the shoulders and shoved him aside. One of the muscular young men Metwater kept near him as bodyguards rushed forward, but Jake ignored him and charged into the bedroom. Carmen followed, one hand hovering over the weapon under her skirt. She didn't want to blow her cover by drawing the gun, but Jake might not leave her any choice.

Phoenix lay on Metwater's bed and, with her whitish hair and her face so pale, she almost blended with the sheets. As Jake reached her, the bodyguard grabbed his arm. "No!" Phoenix sat up, one arm outstretched. "Don't hurt him, please!"

Jake's thunderous expression softened. He sat on the edge of the bed and took Phoenix's hand. "Hello, Mom."

Her smile transformed her face. "Jake. What a wonderful surprise!" She cupped his face in her hands, as if needing to reassure herself he was real. "What are you doing here?"

"I came to see you. How are you feeling?"

"I'm fine." She managed a wavering smile. "I just got too hot out there or I didn't drink enough water or something." She wrapped both of her hands around his. "It's so good to see you. How did you ever find me?"

"It wasn't easy," he said. "I talked to a lot of people. One of your old friends from Denver mentioned you'd taken up with some millionaire turned preacher. I did some more digging and heard about this group and came out here to see if you were with them."

"I kept meaning to write and let you know Sophie and I were okay and that you shouldn't worry. You always were such a worrier."

"You shouldn't disappear that way," Jake said. "What were you thinking?"

Phoenix licked her pale lips. "Do your grandparents know I'm here?" she asked.

"No. Not yet."

She lay back on the pillows and closed her eyes. "Don't tell them, please. There's really no need for them to know."

He looked as if he wanted to argue that point but pressed his lips together and said nothing.

Metwater moved to the other side of the bed and took Phoenix's hand. "What are you doing here?" he asked Jake.

"I came to see my mother."

"This is my son." Opening her eyes, Phoenix struggled to a sitting position once more. "Jake, this is the Prophet. The man who saved my life." She beamed at Metwater, the adoration making Carmen a little sick to her stomach. Frankly, the Prophet, for all his good looks and charm—or possibly because of them—gave her the creeps.

"You need to leave now," Metwater said. "You're obviously upsetting your mother."

"Oh, no!" Phoenix protested. "We haven't even had a chance to talk. And I'm feeling much better, I promise." She started to get out of bed, but Metwater pushed her back against the pillows once more.

"I can feel your pulse racing," he said. "All this excitement isn't good for you." He turned to Jake. "You can see your mother later. Tomorrow, after she's had a chance to rest."

"Or I could take her with me now," he said. "To a doctor who can check her out. Someplace safe."

"Jake, I don't need a doctor," Phoenix protested. "And why wouldn't I be safe here? The Prophet has given me his own bed. I don't deserve such an honor."

"Mother, I came to take you away from here. You and Sophie."

Carmen winced. Not the way to approach this.

Phoenix laughed. "Don't be silly, Jake. This is my home. Our home. We're not going anywhere."

"That's right," Metwater said. He smiled and beckoned toward Sophie. "Come here, child. Don't be shy."

Sophie flushed and walked very slowly, head down, to the side of the bed where Metwater sat. He put his arm around her and pulled her close. "You're happy here, aren't you?" he asked, his lips practically brushing the girl's cheek.

She stood frozen, avoiding his eyes.

"Of course she's happy." Phoenix stroked her daughter's hand. "You love it here, don't you, dear?"

Sophie nodded, though she still didn't look up. Carmen swallowed the sour taste in her mouth. She had to fight to keep from ordering Metwater to take his hands off the girl. The muscles bunched along Jake's jaw as he glared at the Prophet.

Metwater met the glare with a challenging look of his own. "Your mother and sister are well cared for here," he said. "You don't have anything to worry about."

Carmen wasn't so sure about that. She couldn't decide whether Daniel Metwater or Jake Lohmiller was likely to cause the most trouble.

Jake glared at Metwater. "Get your hands off my sister," he said, and there was no mistaking the menace behind his words.

"Sophie doesn't mind, does she?" Metwater snuggled the girl closer.

"Get your hands off her, or I'll break them off!"

"Jake!" Phoenix grabbed his arm. "That's no way to talk to a holy man."

"There's nothing holy about the way he's holding Sophie."

Phoenix sent her daughter a worried look. "Maybe Sophie should leave us now," she said.

Metwater unwrapped his arms from around the girl. "You may go now, daughter," he said.

Sophie ran from the room without looking at any of them. A moment later, the door to the motor home slammed behind her.

Phoenix turned to Jake. "Now look what you've done," she said.

"What *I've* done?" Jake stood. "This charlatan has pulled the wool over everyone's eyes. Can't you see this is no place for a child? This is no place for you."

"Enough." Metwater clapped his hands together. "You may not come into my home and insult me this way."

Jake took a step toward the Prophet, fists clenched. Carmen had seen enough. She moved forward and took his arm. "Come with me," she said softly. "We'll figure something out."

"You're not welcome in my home or my Family's home," Metwater said. "Leave, and don't come back."

The guard stepped forward and took Jake's other arm. His muscles tensed beneath Carmen's hand, but she held on, even as he shook off the guard. "I'm leaving," he said. "But this isn't the last you've seen of me."

Chapter Three

Jake wrenched from Carmen's grasp and stalked out of the room. She started after him, but Metwater's voice stopped her. "How do you know this man?" he asked.

"I don't," she said. "He approached me while we were out gathering fruit. He told me he was Phoenix's son and that he wanted to see her. Then Sophie ran up and told us her mother had collapsed."

"It was just too much sun," Phoenix protested. "I'm fine." She looked to Metwater. "Jake always did have a hot temper, but he doesn't mean anything by it. He's a good boy. He was just worried about me, that's all."

Metwater kept his gaze fixed on Carmen. He had dark, piercing eyes that dared you to blink first. "I don't want you associating with him," he said. "He strikes me as dangerous."

Carmen nodded. Not that she was agreeing with Metwater, but she was anxious to get out of the motor home and find Jake before he caused any more trouble.

"You may go now," Metwater said.

She ground her teeth together. Reminding him she didn't need his permission to walk away wouldn't fit with her cover of the new, meek disciple. She kept her head down until she was out of the RV, then looked around for Jake.

She spotted him with Starfall and another woman, Sarah, outside a lean-to that served as the camp's communal kitchen. "We were just telling Soldier Boy here that we could use a man like him around," Starfall said. She gave Jake an appreciative once-over.

"Your Prophet doesn't agree," Jake said.

"He doesn't like people who disagree with him," Sarah said. When the others looked at her, she flushed. "But it's his camp, so I guess he gets to make the rules."

"Phoenix never let on she had a good-looking son like you," Starfall said, looking Jake up and down.

"She doesn't talk about her past," Sarah said. "Most people here don't."

"They don't," Starfall agreed. She turned to Carmen. "For instance, we don't know anything about Carmen here, except that she heard the Prophet at a rally in Grand Junction and fell in love with his teachings."

"There's nothing to know," Carmen said. She touched Jake's arm. "Where is Sophie?"

"I don't know." He frowned. "I need to find her."

"She's probably at Phoenix's trailer," Starfall said.

"You know teenagers. They're always in a snit about something."

"I'll take you there," Carmen said.

Jake followed her away from the two women. When they were out of earshot, Carmen said, "We have to hurry. Metwater will send someone to make sure you left camp, and Starfall will probably tell them where you went."

"Does everyone here do what Metwater tells them to do?" he asked.

"That's part of the deal when you join up with his *Family*," she said. "You turn over all your worldly goods to him and agree to live by his rules."

"You did that?" he asked.

"No. I'm still on probation. I get to hang around for a couple of weeks and decide if this is what I really want."

Jake looked around them. Women and children were everywhere, along with a handful of men. Everyone was young and attractive. "I don't get it," he said. "What do people see in this kind of life?"

"They're unhappy and looking for something," she said. "Some meaning or purpose. They want to be part of a special group and feel special themselves. Metwater promises that."

His eyes, as intense as the Prophet's, met hers, but with a warmth she had never found in Metwater's gaze. "What does he get out of it?" he asked.

"All their property, for one thing, though for most

of them that's just a little cash and maybe a vehicle. A lot of adoration and ego strokes. Power."

"And nothing he's doing is against the law?"

She shrugged. "As long as the people involved are competent adults and they hand over everything willingly, there's not a lot we can do."

"Which brings me back to my original question," he said. "Why are you here?"

She glanced around, as much to buy time to formulate her answer as to make sure they couldn't be overheard. "There are a lot of women and children here. We want to make sure there's no abuse involved."

He stiffened. "Have there been reports of abuse? Rumors?"

"No." She pressed her lips together. "It just seems the potential is there. We wanted to be sure."

"*We* being what organization? Child Protective Services?"

"No. The CPS is satisfied that everything is fine here." He had already pegged her as a cop—her refusal to acknowledge that hadn't changed his mind. Maybe it was better to let him know she had real authority behind her. "I work for the Ranger Brigade."

He considered this. "That's a federal group, right? Multi-agency take force working on public lands? I think I read something in the paper about you. But there can't be many people out here. Is there much crime?"

"You might be surprised. People think they can

get away with a lot when there aren't many people around to watch."

"But you're watching," he said. "What crimes do you think Daniel Metwater and his bunch are committing?"

"Why should I tell you? I don't know anything about you."

"You know my name. You know I'm a veteran."

"What have you been doing since you were discharged from the Army?" she asked.

"I've been looking for my mother and my sister. And I just want to protect them. If you know something about Daniel Metwater that bears on that, please tell me."

The man was either an Emmy-worthy actor, or he was being straight with her. He had already had the chance to blow her cover and hadn't done so, and his concern for his mother and sister was genuine. Maybe he could even help her in some way, if she gave him a little more information.

"He hasn't done anything that we can link directly to him," she said. "But he attracts the kind of people who bring trouble. A couple of weeks ago, we arrested a serial killer who was one of his hangers-on. Not a follower, exactly, but someone who visited the camp often and was close to Metwater. There have been other incidents around the camp." She shook her head. "I shouldn't even be talking about this. I'm on really thin legal ground here. The local DA has asked us to back off. Metwater's lawyers have accused us of targeting the group and harassing Metwater and his followers."

"But you're federal, right? You don't have to comply with the DA's orders?"

"Right. But we're trying to keep things low-key. I'm here to compile a census of the group and to make sure everything is above-board." Not exactly a dangerous undercover mission.

"And he was really harboring a serial killer?" He shook his head. "All the more reason to get Sophie and my mother out of here."

They had reached the turquoise and white vintage travel trailer Sophie shared with her mother. "I don't think your mother and sister are in any danger," Carmen said.

"You saw the way Metwater held Sophie. The guy's a creep."

"Yes. It was…unsettling. But as free as he is with the women in camp, I've never seen him make any kind of unhealthy gesture toward the children. And that includes Sophie. He refers to all the children as his own. And I'm watching him very closely."

Jake looked over the trailer. "So this is where they live?"

"It's really very comfortable inside," Carmen said. "I'm sure Sophie will be happy you came after her."

She started to turn away, but he touched her arm. "Will you come with me?"

The request surprised her. "I would have thought you wanted to see your sister alone."

He grimaced. "Until a few moments ago, we hadn't seen each other in four years. The last time I saw her she was just a little kid. Now…" He shrugged. "I'm not sure I know what to say to her. It might be less awkward with you along."

This was the first chink in his armor he had shown, and it touched her. "All right." Maybe hearing what he had to say to his sister would help her figure him out.

Jake knocked on the door, but there was no answer. "Sophie, it's me, Jake," he called. "Can I come in?"

The door opened, and Sophie peered out at them, her expression wary. "What do you want?" she asked.

"I just want to see you," he said. "It's been a long time."

She looked past him to Carmen. "All right," she said and held the door open wider.

The little trailer was crowded but neat, despite Sophie's schoolbooks scattered across the dinette table and the kitchen counter covered with jars of dried herbs, a bowl of the wild raspberries they had picked that morning and a tin can filled with purple and yellow wildflowers. "Are you okay?" Jake sat on a small sofa next to his sister.

"Sure." She shrugged. "I'm just worried about Mom."

"Has she fainted like this before?" Carmen asked.

"A couple of times—" Sophie worried her lower

lip between her teeth "—that I know about. And she's been tired a lot lately."

"When was the last time she saw a doctor?" Carmen asked.

"She doesn't believe in doctors," Sophie said.

"I'll talk to her and see what I can find out," Carmen said.

Sophie brightened. "That would be great. She won't say anything to me 'cause, you know, I'm just a kid."

"Did that guy, Metwater, upset you?" Jake asked.

Her expression clouded once more. "You upset me. Going all caveman and arguing over me like I was, I don't know, a dog or something. It was embarrassing."

Jake looked at Carmen, desperation in his eyes. "I wasn't trying to embarrass you," he said. "I didn't like the way he was holding you. I didn't think you liked it, either."

"I don't like him because he keeps saying he's my father now and stuff like that."

"He hasn't ever, like, touched you, um, inappropriately, has he?" The tips of Jake's ears were red, but he marshaled on. "You know what I'm talking about, right?"

"Yes, I know." Sophie looked miserable. "And he hasn't done anything like that. I'd call him on it if he did. I'm not afraid of him like some of the people around here."

"Why are they afraid of him?" Carmen asked.

"Well, maybe *afraid* isn't the right word. Mom is just in awe of him and thinks he really is this holy man. And he has those bodyguards he orders around to enforce his rules, so I guess that makes some people nervous."

"What kind of rules?" Jake asked.

"Oh, just stuff like you're not supposed to have guns in camp, and we don't eat meat on Mondays and Fridays—stuff like that. It's no big deal."

"What did Mom mean when she said Metwater had saved her life?" Jake asked.

"He got her off heroin. I thought you knew that."

"I wasn't sure she was off," Jake said.

"She is." Sophie looked around. "I mean, where is she going to score drugs out here? Anyway, the Prophet got her to quit, and he gave her her new name." She looked at Carmen. "She was Anna before. Now she's Phoenix. You know, that mythical bird that rose from the ashes. Mom loves that kind of thing."

"I take it Grandma and Grandpa don't know where you are," Jake said.

Sophie's eyes widened. "No, and you can't tell them."

"Why not?"

"Because the court awarded them custody of me, back when Mom was still doing drugs—right after you left to join the military."

Jake scowled. "Why didn't anyone tell me about this?"

"I don't know. I guess because you and Mom argued before you went away, and she figured you would side with Grandma and Grandpa against her."

"She was probably right," he said. "If you were with Grandma and Grandpa now, you'd be living in a real house and going to school and having friends your own age."

"And where would Mom be? If you make me go live with Grandma and Grandpa, she'll be all alone."

"Sophie, it isn't your job to look after Mom," he said. "She's supposed to look after you."

"She's doing that. We're fine here."

"Except you're hiding from our grandparents."

Sophie pushed her lips out in a pout. "I don't want to live with them. I want to stay with Mom."

"Then she should go to court and get legal custody of you. I could even help you with that."

Sophie looked skeptical. "Mom would never do that. She hates lawyers and cops and people like that."

"A lot of times people like that are on your side," he said. "Don't ever be afraid to go to the police if you need help." His gaze met Carmen's over the top of Sophie's head and a warm thrill ran through her. She really didn't want to like this guy as much as she was starting to—not when she still had so many unanswered questions about him.

"Promise me you won't tell Grandma and Grandpa we're here," Sophie said.

Jake looked stubborn. "Mom is breaking the law by keeping you here with her," he said.

"You don't understand!" Sophie's face twisted, the picture of teenage angst. "Mom needs me."

Carmen put a steadying hand on the girl's shoulder. "Your brother is just trying to understand the situation." She gave Jake a hard look. He needed to tone it down and stop putting Sophie on the defensive. "He wants what's best for you *and* your mom."

"Of course I do." His smile looked a little forced, but Carmen appreciated that he was trying. "I want you both safe and happy."

"We're safe and happy here."

Jake opened his mouth as if to argue but wisely thought better of it. Instead, he stood. "I'll come back to see you as soon as I can," he said.

"Promise?" Sophie's eyes were shiny, as if she was holding back tears. "You won't leave us again, will you?"

"No, I won't leave." He gave her a last, desperate look before leaving.

"Will you be all right here by yourself?" Carmen asked Sophie. "You can come stay with me if you like." The tent she had brought with her wasn't that big, but she would make room for the girl.

"Mom will be back soon." Sophie smoothed her hand over the seat cushion. "She's going to be all right, isn't she?"

"We'll make sure of it." Carmen gave the girl's shoulder another reassuring squeeze. She was so young and trying to be so strong. Carmen wanted to pull her into her arms and hold her tight, but she sensed Sophie would resist. After all, Carmen was a stranger to her, and the life she had led so far had probably taught her not to trust strangers. She wasn't even sure she could trust her brother.

"Will you talk to Jake?" Sophie asked. "Convince him that Mom and I are fine here. We don't want to go back to Grandma and Grandpa."

"Why don't you want to go back to them?" Carmen asked.

"Because Mom is happy here. Her old friends and the drugs and everything aren't here. She's safe here. I want her to be safe."

"I'll talk to him," Carmen said. "But I doubt he'll listen to me." Jake struck her as a man who made up his own mind, without relying on the opinions of others.

"He likes you," Sophie said. "That will make him listen."

Carmen might have argued with that but let it pass. "You come to me if you need anything," she said and left the little trailer.

Jake was waiting outside, frowning at a couple of men who were watching him from beneath a tree across the clearing. "More of Metwater's goons?" he asked, as Carmen came up beside him.

Carmen studied the two shaggy-haired young men, boyfriends of a couple of the women she had met. "They're not part of his bodyguards," she said.

"But they've probably heard you're not supposed to be in camp."

"Maybe I should hang around a little longer, to show Metwater what I think of his trying to order me around," he said.

"Don't." She gripped his arm. "You're not going to help your sister and mother by raising a stink like this. Let me handle this. I promise I'll make sure Phoenix and Sophie are all right."

His eyes met Carmen's, and the intensity of his look burned into her. "Looking after them isn't your job," he said. "It's mine. And it's my fault they're here right now. If I had stayed home, instead of leaving them to run off to the military, Sophie would be safe in Houston with our grandparents. She'd be enrolled in school and worrying about boys her own age, instead of living here in the wilderness with a phony prophet and his whacked-out followers."

"Or maybe things would be worse, and your mother would still be an addict or dead of an overdose." She faced him, toe to toe. "You won't accomplish anything playing the blame game."

He clenched his jaw. "You're right. But I'm not going to let you or Metwater or anyone else keep me from looking after Sophie and my mom now."

"Where is Sophie's father?" Carmen asked.

"Who knows? He was another free spirit Mom hooked up with for a few months during one of the periods when I was living with my grandparents.

He's a musician out in California—a real flake. I think he's seen Sophie twice in her whole life."

"That must be hard on her." Carmen saw her own father at least once a week.

"Probably, but you adjust."

The tension in his voice tugged at her. "Who was your father?" she asked.

"Another guy who ran out on her when she needed him," Jake said. "A high school classmate— apparently a senior who was headed to college. His plans didn't include her and a kid." He shrugged. "I never met him. Never wanted to."

Was that true? Carmen wondered. Surely a boy would want to know his father. Her own dad was an anchor in her life, a source of love and guidance and so many qualities that made her who she was. Being rejected by a parent must have hurt Jake deeply, even though he didn't show it. "None of you have had it easy, then," she said.

His jaw tightened. "We did all right. Most of the time. And I'm going to take care of Mom and Sophie now."

"There's nothing more you can do today," she said. "You should go before there's trouble."

"I'll leave camp—for now. But I promise, I'll be keeping an eye on this place—and on you."

He turned and stalked away, leaving her breathless in the wake of this pronouncement, a feeling curling up from her stomach that was part fear and part attraction she really, really didn't want to feel.

Chapter Four

Jake hiked back to his camp in a secluded copse, just off a dirt road. The sun beat down, hot on the top of his head. A soft breeze brought in the smells of sage and pinion, and the trill of birds. Such a peaceful, idyllic scene. Some of Metwater's followers probably saw it as a kind of Eden. The Prophet no doubt painted it that way. But Jake sensed something rotten underneath all that beauty.

Carmen must have sensed it, too. He wasn't sure if he bought her story about being undercover in the camp to check on the conditions for the women and children. Why carry concealed if you were only doing a welfare check?

He hadn't made her as a cop when he'd first seen her, walking with the women. Did that make him sexist? Or was it only because his attraction to her had sidetracked his thinking? Her cool, reserved attitude intrigued him. He liked that she didn't rattle easily, and he'd be a liar if he didn't admit that her slightly exotic beauty added to her appeal. She was the type of woman he'd want guarding his back in a fight—and by his side in bed.

The odds weren't good either of those things would happen. Officer Redhorse didn't trust him— not even to look after his own mom and sister. Maybe her instincts were better than his, and she sensed he wasn't entirely leveling with her. But he had plenty of good reasons for keeping secrets just now.

In any case, he didn't have room in his life for a relationship right now—he hadn't had that kind of room for a long time. Before the army, family drama had stolen all opportunity to get close to anyone else. He'd been caught between his concern for his mom and sister, and his anger that they were always so needy. His mother was over forty, and she seemed incapable of looking after herself. She was always in trouble—trouble with creditors, trouble with the law, trouble with drugs.

Four years ago, he had told himself things weren't that bad. His leaving might even be the kick in the pants she needed to accept her responsibilities and get clean. When he had finally gotten over his anger enough to touch base with her, six months after he'd enlisted, he had been more annoyed than worried when he discovered she had left town. He told himself she would turn up again. She always did.

Then he had been deployed, and time had gotten away from him. It had taken him months after his discharge to find her, months during which he had decided he had been a coward for running out on Sophie the way he had. He had been so eager to escape his problems, he hadn't thought of anyone else. The knowledge hurt, like a punch in the gut. He wouldn't make that mistake again. He wouldn't let her down this time.

He approached the camp he had made in a secluded wash, screened from the road by a tumble of red and gray boulders and a clump of twisted pinions. He froze when he spotted the Jeep parked next to his pickup, secluded behind some trees. He doubted anyone had accidentally chosen that place to park. As carefully and soundlessly as possible, he reached back and eased the gun out of his pack, then unfastened the pack's straps and let it slip to the ground.

Unencumbered, he moved stealthily toward the camp, keeping out of sight behind the screen of boulders. Warmth from the rocks seeped into his palm as he braced himself to look through a gap into the camp.

An older man with a barrel chest, dressed in khaki shorts and a white, short-sleeved shirt that billowed over his big belly, bent over to peer into Jake's tent. When he straightened, Jake studied the jowled face with mirrored aviators perched on a bulbous nose. This guy was no cop—he didn't have that aura about him, and he was seriously out of shape. Jake could hear him wheezing from across the camp.

The man spotted the cooler that Jake had shoved deep into the shade of a pinion and waddled over to it and popped the top. Smiling, he pulled out a beer, condensation glinting on the brown glass. Nope, not a cop. Just a common thief. Jake rose from behind the rock, his gun trained on the intruder. "Put that back where you got it," he barked.

The man inhaled sharply, and the bottle slipped from his hand, shattering on the rock below, beer fountaining up and onto the man's hiking boots. He looked down at the mess, frowning. "Shame on you for making me waste a good beer," he said in heavily accented English. Was he German? Austrian?

"What are you doing in my camp?" Jake asked.

"I was looking around." The man was red-faced from too much sun, but he didn't look nervous.

"And you were helping yourself to my beer," Jake said.

"I was thirsty. Isn't that the rule of the outdoors—to always offer refreshment to a fellow traveler in need?"

Jake took a step closer, keeping the gun trained on the intruder. "You don't walk into someone's camp and help yourself. That's called theft."

The man spread his hands in front of him. "I did not mean to offend. Perhaps things are done differently here in the wild west of America." He nodded toward Jake's gun. "You are making me nervous, waving that around."

"Keep your hands where I can see them, and turn around."

The man hesitated. "Why do you ask this?"

"I'm not asking. Do it."

The man slowly raised his hands and turned to present his back. Jake moved from behind the rock and checked the man's pockets and waistband. No gun. He relaxed a little and lowered his weapon, though he kept it in his hand. "You can turn around now."

The man did so. Up close, he looked even older—close to sixty. "What are you doing out here?" Jake asked.

"I am on vacation."

"From where?"

"From Germany. Munich. I come to the United States every year."

Jake looked around at the austere landscape. Not the kind of thing he would expect a city guy from Munich to be attracted to. "Why?"

"I embrace the wild beauty of this land." The German spread his arms wide. "I find it endlessly fascinating."

"Really?"

He dropped his hands. "Also, I have a great interest in the flora and fauna of the American wilderness."

"Are you a botanist or something?"

"I am a hobbyist. My name is Werner Altbusser." He extended his hand, but Jake didn't take it. He didn't for a minute believe this guy was as innocent as he pretended to be.

"Where are you camped?" Jake asked.

If he had been on the receiving end of these questions, Jake would have told the guy his campsite was none of his business, but Werner had no such qualms. "I am staying in a motel in Montrose," he said. "I do not enjoy camping. And I realized when I was out here that I had not brought enough water with me, hence I was doubly glad to see your camp."

Werner hadn't just "seen" Jake's camp. Jake had made sure it wasn't visible from the road, and there were no nearby trails. "So you figured you'd wander over and take a look," Jake said.

"I hoped someone would be home, and I could ask for a drink."

Jake opened the cooler and took out a bottle of water. "Here you go."

If the German was disappointed not to receive a beer, he didn't show it. He twisted the lid off the water bottle and half drained it in one gulp. So maybe he was thirsty. Jake took out a bottle of water for himself.

Thirst slaked, Werner looked around the camp. "This is a remote location," he said. "What brings you here? Are you, like me, a lover of nature?"

"I have business in the area."

Werner's eyebrows arched in unspoken question, but Jake didn't elaborate.

"I met some other people camped in the area," Werner said. "A group of young people, who said they are part of a large family who live here."

Jake stiffened. Was he talking about Metwater's bunch? "Where did you meet them?" he asked.

"Oh, while I was out walking." He waved his hand vaguely. "Very nice young people." He grinned, showing white teeth. "Very pretty women. Do you know them?"

"No," Jake lied.

Werner drained the rest of the bottle, then crumpled it and set it on top of the cooler. "Thank you for the water. I will be going now."

Jake couldn't think of a good reason to detain the man. "Next time you come across an unoccupied camp, don't wander in and help yourself," he said. "The next person you meet might not be as understanding as me," he said.

"I will remember that." He gave a small bow, then turned and walked unhurriedly to the Jeep. After a few moments, the engine roared to life and trundled back to the road.

Jake waited until the vehicle was out of sight, then retrieved his pack and carried it into his tent. Out of habit, he checked the contents, searching through the spare shirt and socks, extra ammo, energy bars, sunscreen and water. But the item he was looking for wasn't there.

He upended the pack on his sleeping bag, and emptied out the side pockets as well, the sinking feeling in his stomach growing to Grand Canyon proportions. The folder with his credentials and badge were gone. Whoever had taken them now knew he was a Fish and Wildlife officer. His cover was blown before the sting had even begun.

Chapter Five

Starfall cornered Carmen after breakfast the next day. "Heard from Soldier Boy?" she asked, smirking.

Carmen started to pretend she didn't know who Starfall was talking about, but why play dumb? "I haven't heard from him," she said.

"Hmm." Starfall twirled one long curl around her index finger. "I was hoping he'd stop by today to visit."

"You know the Prophet told him he wasn't welcome here." Metwater had made a point after dinner last night of announcing that he wanted everyone to be more vigilant about keeping out uninvited visitors. He passed it off as a concern for the safety of the group, though he had specifically mentioned Jake as an example of someone who could disrupt the harmony of the group.

"Roscoe said he spotted a bunch of berry bushes south of here," Starfall said. Roscoe was the Family's mechanic. He made extra money by collecting rusting metal and the remains of cars that had been dumped in the wilderness, and selling them to scrap dealers in town. "Want to come pick with us this morning? If we get enough fruit, we can make jam."

Carmen actually liked picking berries. The weather was pleasant, the scenery beautiful and it was one of her best opportunities to mingle with all of the women and many of the children in the group. She was learning about their backgrounds and getting a good picture of their relationships to the Prophet and to each other. Though some of them looked a little more ragged and dirty than others, she hadn't found any real signs of neglect. A little more attention to schooling and health care would have been warranted, but she couldn't see that Metwater and his followers were breaking any laws. Another day or two, and she would have to wrap up her investigation and get back to more pressing matters, so she might as well make the most of the time she had left. "Sure, I'll come."

When the women assembled with their buckets and baskets, Carmen was surprised to see Sophie and Phoenix. "Are you sure you're well enough to be going out?" she asked Phoenix.

"I told her she should stay home and rest," Sophie said.

"I'm fine." Phoenix smiled. She looked pale but, then, she always looked pale. "And I like berry picking. I wouldn't want to stay behind and miss it."

"Come on, let's go," Starfall called. "I don't want to wait around all morning."

They set out, a motley collection of half a dozen women and an equal number of children. Some women had chosen to remain behind, including Asteria. But most enjoyed the opportunity to be away from camp, enjoying the nice weather. They found the raspberry bushes Roscoe had told them about, the thorny, fruit-laden canes clustered along the edge of a small canyon. Carmen began filling a plastic ice-cream bucket with the sweet, red fruit, careful to avoid the sharp thorns which continually caught and tugged on her clothes. She had worn jeans for the work and a billowing blouse that hid the gun tucked into her waistband.

Except for the gun, she was reminded of other berry-picking expeditions when she was a girl, with her relatives on the Southern Ute Reservation south of here. Aunt Veronica would try to scare them with stories about bears that would try to steal the fruit, and her mother would promise a reward for the child who picked the most berries. Smiling at the memory, Carmen paused to stretch her back and sample some of the juicy berries. She was sucking juice from her fingers when she noticed Starfall had moved away from the others and was searching the ground some distance away.

While most of the women had welcomed Carmen to the Family, Starfall had kept her distance. Carmen was still trying to figure out where the slight, curly-haired woman fit into the group dynamic. She wasn't one of Metwater's favorites—women who hovered

around him at every meal and ceremony, like groupies around a rock star. She shared a tent with Asteria
next to Metwater's motor home and had a little boy
whose father had accompanied her to the Family, but
who had left after less than a month. All this Carmen
had learned from other women, not Starfall herself.
There was something sly and grasping about the young
woman that made Carmen always on edge around
her—and curious to know what she was hiding.

She moved away from the berry pickers and toward Starfall. The other woman straightened at her
approach. "What are you looking for?" Carmen
asked.

Starfall swept her mass of curly, brown hair back
from her forehead. "Do you know anything about
cactus?" she asked.

"Not much." Her grandmother had taught her how
to cook the green pads of prickly pear—removing
the thorns and cutting the flesh into thin strips to
sauté as a vegetable—but it wasn't one of Carmen's
favorite dishes, and she doubted Starfall was interested in the recipe.

"I'm looking for this." Starfall thrust a piece of
paper toward her. Carmen took the paper and studied it. Obviously printed from the internet, it showed
a squat, barrel-shaped cactus with wicked-looking
spines and a soft pink flower.

"Where did you get this?" Carmen asked, returning the paper.

Starfall folded the copy and tucked it in the pocket

of her skirt. "I met a guy in town who said he'd pay me twenty bucks for every one of these I found and brought to him." She studied the ground again. "He said they grew around here, but they wouldn't have flowers this time of year."

"Isn't it against the law to take plants from public land?" Carmen asked. She knew it was, though enforcement was lax, considering the other crimes the Rangers had to worry about.

"This place is full of cactus," Starfall said. "Who's going to miss one?"

"Who was this guy?" Carmen asked, joining Starfall in searching the ground.

"Some old German. A tourist. He said he collects cactus. It sounded like an easy way to earn twenty bucks. But maybe not. I've been looking all morning and haven't seen any of these."

"Starfall!"

Sophie ran to them. "I think I found one of those cactus you're looking for," the girl said.

"Really?" Starfall brightened. "Show me."

Carmen followed the two of them to a spot near the canyon rim but away from the berry thicket. Sophie squatted down and pointed. "It's not very big," she said. "But it looks like your picture."

Starfall pulled out the paper and held it beside the cactus. "I think you're right." She patted Sophie's shoulder. "Thanks, honey." She straightened, then put up her hand to shield her eyes as she stared in the distance. A sly smile spread across her face. "Well, what do you know?"

Carmen followed the other woman's gaze and recognized the tall figure striding toward them, just as Sophie shouted "Jake!" and began running toward her brother.

Jake hugged Sophie, then the two continued arm in arm toward Carmen and Starfall.

"What are you all looking at?" he asked when he joined them.

"Why, you, Soldier Boy," Starfall said, while Carmen said nothing.

"Hello, Carmen," he said.

"Hello." She kept her expression and her voice cool. She still hadn't made up her mind how she felt about Jake. On one hand, she admired his devotion to his sister and mother, and his courage and determination to do the right thing. But he also struck her as quick-tempered and a little mysterious. She appreciated a strong man, but she didn't want to have to wonder if he was on the right side of the law.

"I told Mom you'd come back," Sophie said.

"Where is she?" Jake looked past his sister toward the other women, who had moved down the rim of the wash to pick more berries.

"I talked her into sitting down under a tree and resting." Sophie pointed to a shady spot where Phoenix sat. Just then, the older woman looked over to them, smiled and waved.

"How is she feeling today?" Jake asked.

"She says she's better." Sophie shrugged. "I guess she is. She came back to the trailer about suppertime and went straight to bed and slept all night, so maybe she was just really tired."

"Uh-huh."

"What brings you to see us, Soldier Boy?" Starfall lightly touched Jake's shoulder and smiled.

"I was out hiking and saw you all picking berries and thought it would be a good opportunity to visit with my mom and sister away from the camp."

"You're not afraid of the Prophet's enforcers, are you?" Starfall said. She squeezed his bicep. "You look like a man who knows how to handle himself."

Jake shrugged away from her. "What were you ladies looking at just now?" he asked.

"We were looking at cactus," Sophie said, ignoring Starfall's frown.

"What kind of cactus?" Jake focused on the ground where Sophie pointed.

"Starfall knows," Sophie said. "Show him the picture."

"I don't think so." Starfall hugged her arms across her chest. "Why don't you go back to your mother, and let us adults talk?"

Sophie pouted. "Jake's my brother. I want to stay with him."

Jake put his arm around her. "Sure, you can stay with me."

Starfall tossed her head. "I was hoping I'd run into you again soon," she said.

"Why is that?" he asked.

She glanced at Carmen. "I wanted to talk to you. Alone."

"You can say whatever you need to say here," he said.

Now it was Starfall's turn to pout. But Jake's expression sent the clear message that he wasn't budging. "I have something that belongs to you," she said. "Something I found when I was out walking yesterday."

He tensed, and it was as if the temperature around him dropped a few degrees. "What is it?" he asked, the three words sharp with anger.

Starfall twirled a lock of hair. "Something you wouldn't want to fall into the wrong hands."

"Give it back."

Sophie cringed at his sharp tone, but Starfall only laughed. "Oh no," she said. "If you want it, you'll have to pay for it. Or I could hand it over to the Prophet. He might be very interested in it."

"What are you talking about?" Sophie asked before Carmen could voice the question.

But neither Jake nor Starfall answered. They glared at each other, then his expression cooled, and he seemed to shrug off his anger. He turned his back to Starfall and squatted to get a closer look at the cactus. It was a clear dismissal. Starfall glared at him, hands fisted at her sides, and Carmen braced herself to pull the other woman off him if she decided to attack.

Jake had to be aware of Starfall's anger, but he continued to ignore her. "I think that's a Colorado hookless cactus," he said to Sophie.

Starfall glared at Carmen, then moved over behind Jake. "Don't you want to know more about this item I found?" she asked.

"Right now I'm more interested in this cactus."

"How does a guy like you know anything about cactus?" she asked.

"It's a hobby of mine."

"That's the same thing the guy said who asked me to find these for him," Starfall said. "Since when are cactus such a big hobby?"

Jake stood. "You might be surprised," he said. "Who was the guy?"

She opened her mouth to answer, but her words were drowned out by the loud *crack!* of gunfire. Granite shards exploded from a nearby boulder. Sophie screamed, and Carmen reached for her weapon but was shoved hard as Jake forced her and Sophie to the ground and then pulled Starfall after them. "Stay down," he ordered, even as he drew a gun.

Chapter Six

Jake fought to slow his breathing and control his racing heart as a second shot struck the dirt in front of the boulder he and the women were sheltering behind. Movement from an outcropping of rock fifty yards distant caught his eye, and he aimed his pistol and fired. No return fire came, and seconds later a car door slammed and an engine roared to life.

Staying low, he moved from behind the boulder and raced in the direction of the shooter's hiding place, cresting a small rise just in time to see the rooster-tail of dust that trailed the vehicle's retreat. Cursing his bad luck, he kept moving toward the rock outcropping where he thought the gunman had been positioned.

He had knelt to examine the area when the pounding of footsteps announced he was not alone. "It's just me," Carmen called before he could raise his weapon once more. She came around the largest boulder, holding her own gun and a little out of breath from running. "Did you get a look at the license plate?" she asked.

He shook his head and shoved his gun back in the waistband of his jeans. "No. And I didn't get a look at him, either." He picked up a stick and nudged a brass casing. "Some of these are still hot."

She moved in beside him, and he caught the clean herbal scent of her hair. "A .223-caliber," she said. "Probably an AR-15."

"That's what I thought," he said. "Pretty common ammo. Tough to trace."

He didn't have to look to know she was pinning him with the kind of gaze designed to make guilty suspects squirm. "What are you doing out here?" she asked.

"I'm here to get my sister and mother away from Metwater, to someplace safer and more suitable for a child."

"And you carry a gun to do it? And what did Starfall mean—she has something of yours? What is she talking about?"

He blew out a breath. He'd known this was coming. In fact, he'd planned to tell her as soon as he had clearance from his supervisors. There wasn't time for that now. He needed help, and she might be the only one he could turn to. He met her gaze with a hard look of his own. "Can I trust you?" he asked.

"I guess that depends on which side of the law you're on."

He liked that answer. "I'm on the right one. I'm a cop, too."

She sat back on her heels, her expression telling him she hadn't seen that one coming. But she recovered quickly. "Let me see your badge."

"That's the problem. I don't have it with me. Someone stole it out of my pack yesterday after I left Metwater's camp. I think it was Starfall."

"How did she manage to steal it out of your pack? What were you doing?"

He checked their surroundings to make sure they couldn't be overheard. Sophie and Starfall were back at the canyon rim, surrounded now by the other women. "Is Sophie okay?" he asked. He had been in such a hurry to pursue the shooter he hadn't had a chance to check on his sister.

"She's fine," Carmen said. "More excited than scared. Tell me how Starfall could have gotten your badge."

"I came back to my camp yesterday after I left you and found an old German guy rifling through my things. I took off the pack and left it on the ground so I could sneak up on him. Starfall must have followed me and gone through the pack while I was dealing with him."

"She said an old German guy was the one who wanted her to collect the cactus for him," Carmen said. "He told her he'd pay her twenty dollars apiece for them."

"They're worth hundreds on the collectible market. Even thousands."

Her eyes widened. "For one little cactus?"

"It's an endangered species. Collectors—especially in Germany and Japan—are fanatics about adding rare specimens to their collections." He stood and offered his hand. After a moment's hesitation, she took it, and he pulled her to her feet.

"Why didn't you show me your badge when I asked you for your ID yesterday?" she asked.

"Because I'm undercover and the fewer people involved the better," he said. "I'm a special agent with the Fish and Wildlife Service. I'm part of a team that has been tracking the German, gathering evidence. He's part of what we suspect is an international team of smugglers. We're hoping he can lead us to some of his partners. When he gets ready to leave the country, we'll confiscate his collection and file charges."

"Where do your mother and sister come in?"

"I volunteered for this job when I learned they needed an agent to come here and follow the German around. I had heard Sophie and my mom might be with Metwater, and this was the perfect opportunity to see if the rumor was true. I had a week's personal time saved up, so I took it before my duties started."

"Are you on the job now?"

"I wasn't supposed to start tracking my suspect for another two days, but obviously he's changed his itinerary and showed up earlier."

"When were you planning to tell the Ranger Brigade about your investigation?" she asked. "You can't operate in our jurisdiction without us knowing about it."

"That part is up to my supervisors, not me," he said. "Though I'm sure you'll tell your bosses about me now."

"I will, but not right away," she said. "Unless there's trouble, I only check in by phone when I can get close enough to town to get a signal."

"You're not worried, being out here on your own?" he asked.

"I told you, this isn't a high-risk assignment. I'm just observing, making sure everything is on the up-and-up with the women and children. Now about your suspect, is he the one who fired on us?"

"I don't know." He looked down at the shell casings again. "This really isn't his style. He hasn't shown any tendency toward violence before."

"And why would he shoot, if he's the one who offered to pay Starfall for the cactus he wanted?" she asked. "Then again, when there's money involved, even passive people can turn mean."

He nodded. "I need to go after him. But I need my badge and credentials. I can't risk them falling into the wrong hands."

"Maybe you should just pay Starfall to give them back."

"I'm not exactly rolling in funds here, and I need the savings I have left to look after Mom and Sophie."

"So, what are you going to do?"

"I was hoping you would help me."

She folded her arms across her chest. "Do you want me to arrest her?"

"Wouldn't that blow your cover?"

"It would. But I'm about done here. I haven't found any evidence of mistreatment of anyone in the camp—by Metwater or anyone else. They aren't living the way most people would probably think is safe and hygienic and all that—but people always said the same thing about Native Americans, and they managed to survive okay." She flashed a smile, her teeth very white against her tanned skin.

"I could arrest her," he said. "But I'd rather use her contact with Werner—the German collector—to build my case against him."

"What do you want me to do?"

"I want you to steal my badge back."

She blinked. "How am I going to do that?"

"You live in that camp. You know where she lives. There can't be many places for her to have hidden something like that."

"And what are you going to do while I'm rifling through her belongings?"

"I'm going to distract her."

"How?"

He shrugged. "She's obviously been flirting with me. Maybe I'll let her think I'm interested."

Did he imagine the spark that fired her eyes at this

suggestion? She looked away before he could be sure. "That would probably work," she said.

"Does that mean you'll help?"

"It's my duty to come to the aid of a fellow law enforcement officer." She spoke with a perfectly straight face, but he thought he caught a glimpse of teasing in her eyes.

"When do you think is the best time to do this?" he asked.

"Tonight. There's a bonfire at dark. Most people are away from their homes then. It would be easier for you to lure her away then, and easier for me to slip into her tent."

"I'll see you tonight, then."

She started to turn away, but he stopped her. "Have you had a chance to talk to my mom about coming with me?" he asked.

"No. She isn't going to listen to me."

He looked past her, toward where his mother and Sophie now sat together in the shade. "I'm going to talk to her. She should at least see a doctor."

"I agree that's a good idea," Carmen said.

A few of the berry pickers looked up when Jake and Carmen approached, but no one said anything as he joined his mother and sister in the shade. He sat beside Sophie and patted her hand. "Are you okay?" he asked.

She nodded. "Who was shooting at us?" she asked.

"I don't know. But they're gone now."

"Maybe it was a poacher who mistook you for a deer," Phoenix said.

Jake could have pointed out that he and the others with him in no way resembled deer or any other game animal, but he kept quiet. If it made his mother feel better to believe the shooting was an accident, he wasn't going to try to dissuade her.

"Too many people have guns who shouldn't," Phoenix said. She scratched her neck. "The Prophet is wise to ban them."

Jake ground his teeth together to keep from telling her what he thought of her Prophet. "How are you feeling today?" he asked instead. "Did something bite you?"

She stopped scratching. "It's nothing. And I'm feeling much better. I'm sure it was just too much sun yesterday. You see I'm being careful today. I'm staying in the shade and resting."

"Maybe you should see a doctor," he said. "Sophie said this wasn't the first time you've fainted recently."

"Sophie is like you—she worries too much."

"But Mom, I—"

Phoenix waved her hand to cut off her daughter's words. "I'm feeling a little hungry," she said. "Why don't you pick some berries for me?"

Jake could tell Sophie wanted to protest but, after a moment's hesitation, she rose. "I'll come with you," Carmen said and earned a grateful look from the girl.

Phoenix watched them leave. "Carmen is a good

young woman," she said. "She has a very peaceful aura."

Jake wouldn't have described Carmen as *peaceful*. If anything, being around her made him feel more unsettled. "About the doctor, Mom," he prompted.

"I don't need a doctor. I don't trust them."

"If Sophie was sick, you'd take her to the doctor, wouldn't you?" he asked.

"Sophie is never sick. We live a very healthy life here. Much healthier than if we lived in the city."

"But you obviously aren't well. Well people don't faint for no reason."

"If you think you're going to use my health to try to take Sophie away from me, it isn't going to work." She shoved to her feet and stood glaring down at him. But even this stance failed to make her look strong. She was so small and pale she made him think of a child—or a ghost.

"I don't want to take Sophie away from you," he said gently. "I want us to all be together again. As a family." Not the pretend family Metwater had made in the wilderness but a real one where he could keep her and Sophie safe.

"I want us to be a family, too." She squeezed his hand, excitement lighting her eyes. "I'll ask the Prophet if you can come live with us here," she said. "I know you got off on the wrong foot with him, but I'm sure if you apologize and promise to work on controlling your temper, he'll allow you to stay."

He stiffened and struggled to conceal his annoyance. Hadn't she gotten the message that he didn't want anything to do with her so-called Prophet? "I don't want to stay here," he said. "I don't want to live in the wilderness or follow your Prophet. You need to be where you can have proper medical care—where Sophie can go to school and have friends."

Phoenix released his hand. "We can't leave here," she said. "We have to stay, for Sophie's sake."

"What do you mean?"

"While I was alone with the Prophet yesterday, he told me a secret." She wore a dreamy expression he knew too well—an expression that meant she was caught up in one of her fantasies that had little relation to reality.

"What are you talking about?" he asked.

"You have to promise not to tell Sophie. Not yet."

He said nothing, his eyes locked on hers, tensed for her next words.

"The Prophet told me he wants Sophie to be his wife," she said.

"She's only fourteen!" The words exploded from him and, as several of the others looked in his direction, he forced himself to lower his voice. "That isn't a good thing, Mother. That's one more reason to get her out of here. Why can't you see that?"

"Don't be so reactionary, Jake. He isn't going to marry her right away. He'll wait until she turns eighteen. In the meantime, she can begin studying, learning all the things she needs to know in order to be a good helpmate to him."

"The only thing she needs to learn is how to be a normal teenager. For a grown man to even think of a fourteen-year-old that way is sick."

"No, it's not," Phoenix insisted. "It's a great honor." Her expression grew dreamy again. "Imagine, my daughter married to such an important man."

"No." Jake wouldn't let it happen. Maybe it was too late to save his mother from Daniel Metwater's clutches, but he would protect his sister at all costs.

Chapter Seven

Flames leaped from the pyramid of dry logs, orange light painting eerie shadows across the faces and bodies of the men and women who danced around the bonfire to the hypnotic beat of a deerskin drum. Daniel Metwater, with his chiseled body stripped to a loincloth, and his muscular chest and back gleaming with oil, led the procession of dancers, head thrown back, eyes closed in an expression of either pain or ecstasy—Carmen couldn't tell.

She stepped farther into the shadows, wary of being seen and pulled into the line of dancers. Starfall wasn't dancing, either. Moments before, she had slipped away from the group around the fire, her figure merging with that of a man at the edge of the woods. Jake had shown up right on time— Carmen had recognized his broad shoulders and military stance, even in the dimness. She ignored the churning in her stomach at the sight of the two of them together. Jake was every bit as devious as Starfall, since he hadn't bothered to tell Carmen—

a cop—that he was also law enforcement. And he had stormed off this afternoon after talking to his mother without saying good-bye to her or his sister. So, as far as she was concerned, he and Starfall deserved each other. The only reason she was helping him was because he was a fellow cop. She believed in loyalty to the badge, even if he didn't.

She hurried away from the fire, into the deeper shadows behind the tents and trailers. She moved carefully, guided by memory and instinct more than by the faint light from a quarter moon and the now distant glow of the fire.

The tent Starfall shared with Asteria showed pale in the darkness, a white cocoon illuminated from within by a battery-powered lantern that sat on a TV tray near the tent's entrance. The white-walled tent was the kind favored by hunting outfitters, tall enough to stand and move around in, and big enough to house a crowd for a meal or a poker game. The two women had furnished the space with colorful rugs, cots, a folding table and chairs, and a crib for Starfall's six-month-old son.

Carmen didn't spot a lot of potential hiding places in the sparsely furnished space. She switched off the lamp and made her way to Starfall's cot and dug a small penlight from her pocket. Shielding the light somewhat with her body, she swept the beam over the cot, stopping at the foot of the bed and the metal trunk that sat there.

A black-and-silver padlock secured the hasp of the

trunk. Carmen tugged, but the lock held tight. She added *buy Starfall a new lock* to her list of things to do as she took out a penknife and went to work on the cheap security measure. The lock popped, and Carmen eased up the lid of the trunk.

The items Starfall felt the need to keep under lock and key were pitifully few—a small photo album with old pictures of people Carmen didn't recognize. Her son Hunter's birth certificate shared an envelope with a certificate for someone named Michelle Munson— probably Starfall's real name.

A tattered envelope held a faded Polaroid photo- graph of a little girl with a mass of brown curls— Starfall? With it was a postcard showing a beach scene on one side and a scrawled message on the other. *Hope you're being good for Aunt Stef. Love Mom.* Costume jewelry and old clothing filled most of the rest of the trunk. Carmen found a manila en- velope tucked in the bottom, full of newspaper clip- pings. With a start, she realized the articles were about Daniel Metwater—not Metwater the Prophet, but Metwater the son of a wealthy industrialist. Car- men read through the first article—a description of the finding of his brother David's body. One sen- tence was underlined: *The body was identified by a distinctive tattoo on his left shoulder.*

Why would Starfall be so interested in articles about the Prophet's life before he began his preach- ing? Had she known his brother David? Or was it merely the case of a fan collecting every bit of information she could about her hero?

Carmen replaced the clippings in the envelope and tucked it back into the bottom of the trunk. She felt along the sides and in the lining of the lid, checking for any place Starfall might have hidden Jake's badge and law enforcement ID. She might have slipped it under one of the rugs or sewn it into a tent flap, but neither of those options seemed as secure as a locked trunk.

She replaced everything in the trunk and started to close the lid, then stopped and took out the photo album again. The pink, embossed cover of the album looked old—maybe something Starfall had inherited from someone. The hairstyles and clothing in the pictures inside dated from the 1990s and earlier. The only image Carmen recognized was the eight by ten photo that filled the album's last page. Starfall smiled out from the photo, which might have been a school photo from high school. Carmen turned the page over—it felt heavier and thicker than the others in the album.

She eased her fingers between the photograph and the album page and felt a surge of triumph as she brushed what felt like leather. Working carefully, she snagged the edge and dragged the item out. Bingo! The solemn face of Special Agent Jake Lohmiller looked out at her, across from a gold shield on the other side of the leather folder's crease.

"What are you doing in here, snooping through Starfall's things?"

She slipped the ID into the waistband of her jeans seconds before the flashlight beam lit her up. Pivoting on her heels, she glared at the man who had spoken and shielded eyes with her hand. She could just make out a pale, bearded face and relaxed a little. "Starfall asked me to get something for her," she lied, rising.

"No, she didn't." The speaker, a lean, athletic blond who went by the name Reggae, lowered the flashlight and frowned at her. He was one of a handful of men who hung around the younger women, flirting and offering to do errands, though Starfall usually ignored him.

"Believe me or don't, I don't care." Carmen started to move past him, but he put out a hand to stop her.

"I saw her just now with that new guy—Phoenix's son," he said. "They looked pretty cozy." His scowl told her he wasn't pleased about this.

"Then what are you doing here?" Carmen asked.

"I was waiting for her to come back."

"Why? So you could spy on her and her new boyfriend?"

"You heard the Prophet. That guy isn't supposed to be here. I was going to warn her she could end up in trouble if she let him hang around."

"What kind of trouble?" Carmen asked. Metwater talked about "consequences" for people who disobeyed the rules but, other than kicking them out of the group altogether, what kind of power did he really have over these people?

"I don't know, but it can't be good. The Prophet might make her leave."

"I'll let her know you're concerned." She tried to move past him, but he grabbed her wrist, his grip surprisingly strong.

"Hey!" She tried to pull away, but he held her tight.

"What were you doing in here?" he asked. "And don't lie to me this time."

JAKE HAD NO trouble persuading Starfall to slip off into the woods with him. Was she so trusting, or merely overly confident of her own powers? "I want that badge," he told her when they were out of earshot of the crowd around the bonfire.

"I'm sure you do." She turned toward him and pressed her hand to his chest. "And I'll be happy to give it to you, but you'll have to pay me for my trouble."

"Is that why you took it?" he asked. "For money?"

She moved in closer, her body pressed to his. "I like knowing people's secrets," she said. "I especially wanted to know what makes you tick, Soldier Boy."

"So you went through my pack?"

"It was just lying there." She walked her fingers up his chest. "Finders, keepers."

"The man in my camp—was that the man who asked you to collect cactus for him?"

"What man?" She sounded annoyed. "I didn't see any man. I followed you because I wanted to talk to you. When I saw the pack, I decided to take a look, and I found the badge." She slid her hand around the back of his neck. "I never cared for lawmen before, but for you I could make an exception."

He pulled her hand away. His first instinct was to tell her he had no interest in thieves, but he didn't want to scare her off. He had to keep her occupied until Carmen could get out of the tent. Besides, this might be his best chance to find out more about Werner Altbusser. "How much do you want for the badge?" he asked.

She took a step back. "I figure it ought to be worth at least a thousand dollars to you."

"What if I decide to arrest you instead?"

"I'm a very good liar. I could convince your superiors that you planted the badge on me after I turned down your advances. After all, what competent law enforcement officer loses his badge?"

He winced, grateful she couldn't see him in the dark. He had the feeling this wasn't the first time she had played this particular kind of poker game. He had to be cautious about his next move. He wasn't going to pay her the money. And he wasn't going to arrest her. Doing so would possibly destroy the undercover operation he was assigned to—a project which his agency had spent a great deal of money and time putting together. He had pulled out every persuasive argument he could think of to keep his supervisor from taking him off the case altogether, when he had called in to report his encounter with

Werner in his camp that afternoon. He had managed to convince his bosses that Werner saw him as just another camper, which would make it even easier for Jake to follow him. His supervisor had admitted they had no one else to put on the case right now, but Jake knew if he screwed up again he'd be out—ordered back to Texas and away from Phoenix and Sophie before he could do anything to help them.

Starfall was right—the embarrassment she could deal out to him might be enough to wreck his career.

"I thought the whole point of living in a group like this was that you don't need money," he said. "Everyone pools their resources, and the Prophet provides the rest."

She made a snorting sound. "Everyone needs money. And the Prophet provides what he wants us to have—not necessarily what we need."

"Why are you here if you don't embrace the lifestyle?" he asked.

"I'm getting what I need right now," she said. "And you might be surprised at the opportunities living like this provides a resourceful person."

"Like selling cactus to an old German?" He still hoped she would give him more information about Werner, but she didn't bite.

"Or selling a badge back to a lawman," she said.

"I don't have a thousand dollars on me."

"I can wait. But not long. Bring me the money tomorrow."

"All right. Tomorrow." With a little luck, Carmen would have the badge, and Starfall would be disappointed.

"In the meantime…" She moved in closer. "Sure you don't want to come back to my tent with me?"

"Don't you have a baby to look after?"

"He's staying with Sarah tonight." She smoothed her hand down his arm. "I told her I had plans."

"I'll walk you back, but I won't come in." He needed to make sure Carmen was safely out of there before he let Starfall go in.

"At least give me a chance to change your mind." She took his hand, and he let her lead him back into camp. The bonfire had dwindled to glowing embers, and the drum had long ago fallen silent. No one took note of them as they strolled toward the white tent.

They had almost reached the entrance to the tent when Starfall halted. "I always leave a light burning when I go out at night," she whispered.

"Maybe your roommate came back early and put it out."

"She wouldn't do that." She clutched his arm. "Someone's in there. Don't you see the movement?"

He did see movement. In fact, at that moment, the tent flap flew back, and two people tumbled out. They appeared to be struggling—fighting. Jake pulled a flashlight from his pocket and aimed the beam at the combatants. Carmen was holding onto a skinny blond dude, one arm bent behind his back. "Let me go!" the young man shouted.

"Reggae! What is going on?" Starfall raced forward.

At her approach, Carmen released the young man, who fell forward. She straightened. "Hello, Starfall. Jake."

"She was in your tent," the man said. "She was snooping around in there, and I tried to stop her."

"I was only getting that item you had in your trunk," Carmen said. "The one you needed me to retrieve for you." Her eyes met Jake's, and she gave an almost imperceptible nod. He felt muscles he hadn't even known he'd been tensing relax.

"I didn't ask you to get anything," Starfall said.

"The item you wanted to give to Jake." She lifted the hem of her shirt and pulled a leather folder from the waistband of her jeans and handed it to Jake.

He checked the folder—everything was in order. "Thanks," he said and pocketed the credentials. He wouldn't let them out of his sight again.

"You went through my things!" Starfall charged at Carmen, but Jake caught her around the waist and held her back.

"She took back something you had that didn't belong to you," Jake said.

"I didn't disturb anything else," Carmen said. "And I'll buy you a new lock."

"You can't just go through someone's things," the man—Reggae—said.

Starfall glared at Carmen. "You're going to be

sorry you ever crossed me," she said, then shoved past her into the tent.

Reggae looked after her. "Maybe I should go in," he said. "And, you know, comfort her."

"Why don't you do that?" Jake said. He didn't care one way or another, but he wanted to get rid of the young man.

Reggae lifted the tent flap and ducked in after Starfall. Jake took Carmen's arm. "Let's get out of here while we can," he said.

She looked back over her shoulder as they moved away from the tent. "That didn't go so well."

"Not the best timing," he said. "Now that she knows I'm a cop, she might figure out you're one, too."

"It doesn't matter," she said. "I'm leaving here tomorrow. I didn't find anything useful and I need to get back to more pressing cases."

"Such as?"

She stopped and faced him, moonlight illuminating her face. "I want to help you with your case—if you still have one."

When her eyes met his, he felt a jolt in his gut that had nothing to do with being a cop, but he forced his mind back on work. "Why wouldn't I have a case?"

"Your cover is blown. As soon as Starfall figures out you're tracking Werner, she'll tell the German you're a cop."

"She could, but she's motivated by money. I'm thinking I can get my bosses to agree to pay her as an informant. We can use the evidence she provides to strengthen our case."

"That's taking a big risk," Carmen said.

"I don't think so. I think she's bored. The chance to play secret agent would appeal to her."

"The chance to get closer to you, you mean."

No missing the snide tone in her voice. He suppressed a smile. "Are you jealous?"

"Of course not!" She folded her arms over her chest. "I just know when another woman has her eyes on a man."

And who do you have your eyes on? he thought. "Why do you want to work with me on this case?" he asked.

"If this plant theft and smuggling is on public land, the Rangers should be involved anyway," she said. "In fact, we have an agent working on plant smuggling in the national park."

"We know about that investigation, and that isn't related. This is bigger—international."

"I still want to help you."

"Why?"

"Because I think it's important. And because, if Starfall is involved, she'd give me a remaining link to Metwater's group. I can't be undercover here anymore, but I still want to keep an eye on things. And you'll give me another link through your mother and sister."

"They both like you a lot," he said. "Even if you stop pretending to be one of the Prophet's faithful,

I hope you'll help me persuade my mom to leave here. I think she'll be more inclined to listen to you."

"Maybe not, when she figures out I'm a cop. But I'll do my best to continue to be her friend. And your sister's, too."

"And me?" He moved in closer.

"I'm still trying to figure you out," she said. She rested a hand on his shoulder. "I'm not sure I trust you."

"You can trust me." He slid his arm around her and snugged her closer. "Give me time to prove how much."

She tilted her head up, and he brushed his lips across hers. When she made no protest, he deepened the kiss. She held herself very still at first, as if waiting for him to prove himself. He slid one hand beneath the heavy fall of her hair and savored the heat of her body against his, the softness of her mouth and the earthy, herbal scent of her. The tension left her, and she angled her mouth more firmly against his and tightened her hand on his arm, keeping him with her, though he indicated no desire to leave. She kissed him the way he had seen her do everything else—with strength and confidence and a command of the situation that took his breath away.

She broke off the kiss but held him with a steady gaze. "I'll give you a chance to prove I can trust you," she said.

"You won't be sorry," he said as she stepped away.

"I hope not. Just remember—I don't give second chances."

She walked away. He stared after her until she was no longer visible in the dark, feeling as if he had just been sucker-punched—and wanting to be hit again.

Chapter Eight

Carmen made it back to Ranger headquarters the next morning in time for the commander's briefing. She had packed up her tent and slipped out of camp without saying good-bye to anyone, though she'd left a note, taped to the door of Phoenix's trailer, saying she had decided to go back home but that she hoped to stay in touch. She planned to keep her work as part of the Ranger Brigade secret for as long as possible, since she still hoped to visit the camp to check on Phoenix, Sophie and the others. Once Daniel Metwater and his followers learned she was a cop, he would try to keep her from what he saw as interference with their way of life.

It felt good to be back in uniform, seated at her usual place to the commander's left in the utilitarian conference room. "Welcome back, Sergeant Redhorse," Commander Graham Ellison said after he'd called the meeting to order. "I think we should start with your report."

"To summarize—I didn't find anything actionable at Daniel Metwater's camp," she said. "No signs of abuse or neglect. As far as I could determine, the children and pregnant women in the camp aren't receiving any kind of regular medical care—which we already suspected. But they all appear to be healthy." She frowned, remembering Phoenix's fainting spell and unnatural paleness.

"Why do I sense an 'except' at the end of that statement?" the commander asked.

"There was one incident while I was there—a woman named Phoenix fainted. She didn't look well but insisted she was fine." She shrugged. "You can't force an adult to see a doctor, and I didn't get the sense that Metwater would prevent her from going to a clinic if she wanted to."

"And Andi Mattheson seemed fine to you?" Agent Simon Woolridge asked this question. He had been Carmen's biggest supporter when she had suggested the undercover investigation. A former Emergency Medical Technician, he suspected the young woman who now went by the name of Asteria might be suffering from diabetes or some other complication of her pregnancy and felt the Rangers should intervene.

"She seemed fine," Carmen said. "Though she spent most of her time closeted with Metwater."

"We'll keep an eye on things in the camp, as usual," Graham said. "But for now, we'll turn our attention to other matters."

"Something else did come up while I was at the camp," Carmen said. "It's not related to Metwater.

Only peripherally to one of his family members."
She was about to tell them about Jake and his investigation into cactus smuggling, when a knock on the conference room door interrupted her.

"Come in," Graham called.

One of the administrative assistants stuck her head around the door. "There's someone from Fish and Wildlife here to see you," she said. "He says it's urgent."

"Then you'd better show him in," Graham said.

Carmen wasn't surprised to see Jake Lohmiller step into the conference room. But the sight of him in uniform did give her a jolt. The man she'd first met as a slightly scruffy camper in the backcountry was now the picture of a spit-and-polish officer of the law, from his clean-shaven face and freshly trimmed hair to the gleaming toes of his boots. The combination of authority and sex appeal unnerved her a little more than she wanted to admit.

"Hello." He nodded to the officers gathered around the conference table. "I apologize for interrupting your meeting, but I didn't think this could wait." He stepped toward Graham, who had risen to greet him, and offered his hand. "Special Agent Jake Lohmiller, Fish and Wildlife."

"Graham Ellison, Ranger Brigade." The two men shook hands. "What can we do for you, Agent Lohmiller?"

"I'm working an undercover operation, shadowing a German tourist who is suspected of smuggling thousands of dollars of rare cactus out of the country for sale to collectors in Europe," Jake said. "It's a sensitive case we've been building for more than a year."

"We've had some trouble with plant smugglers in the national park." Lance Carpenter, the Montrose County Sheriff's representative on the Ranger Brigade task force, spoke up. "Not cactus, but ornamental plants. A local landscaper was digging them up without a permit and offering them for sale to customers."

"This case has a much bigger scope," Jake said. "These stolen cactus go to hobbyists, primarily in Germany and Japan, who will pay a premium for wild-gathered rare species. We know, for instance, that this German is targeting the Colorado hookless cactus, which is on the endangered-species list. Its scarcity makes it a prize for collectors. We believe the man I'm following is a fairly low-level player in an international smuggling ring."

"What do you need from us?" Graham asked.

"I've learned that the German is paying locals to dig the cactus for him. If they're caught, they pay the penalty, while he gets away. My assignment is to shadow the German, so I'm asking your help in making contact with these locals."

"Why weren't we made aware of this investigation before now?" Graham asked. Several heads around the table nodded. The Rangers were responsible for law enforcement on public lands, but not every agency believed in sharing information about their cases.

"The fewer people who know about an undercover investigation like this, the safer for everyone," Jake said. "The idea was that I would follow the German and document his activities for the few days he's supposed to be in the area. I'd be in and out before you even knew I was here. But that was before this new development. I contacted my supervisor this morning, and he is supposed to be getting in touch with you."

Graham could have insisted he needed to wait to speak to Jake's supervisor before he agreed to help the Fish and Wildlife agent. Carmen resisted the urge to confirm that his story was legitimate—then she would have to explain how she knew him and why she hadn't mentioned him and his case before now. Never mind that she had been about to tell all before Jake interrupted—it still looked bad.

"I can spare someone for a few days," Graham said. "Lance, since you worked on the other plant-theft case, you can work with Deputy Carpenter."

Carmen ordered herself not to react. Yes, she had wanted to work with Jake on his case, but saying so now would only arouse suspicion about her motives. Since when was she so interested in cactus? And, since every time she and Jake looked at each other she imagined sparks arcing between them, her co-workers might pick up on that. It was tough enough being the only woman on the team, without confirming any suspicions any of the men might have that she was ruled by her emotions. She was as tough as any of them when a case got difficult, but some men always had doubts, and she didn't want to do anything to strengthen those.

"If you don't mind, I'd prefer a woman for the job," Jake said. He avoided looking at Carmen, though she felt as if every other eye in the room was on her. *Way to be subtle*, she thought.

"Why is that?" Graham asked.

"The person the German has contacted to dig cactus for him is a woman. She lives with a group that's camping in the Curecanti Recreation Area—they call themselves *the Family* and are some kind of commune or something."

While the ability to lie was a good talent to have for undercover work, Carmen couldn't help thinking Jake was a little too good at it. What was wrong with admitting he knew Metwater and his followers? Or was it simply ingrained in him to never reveal more information than he had to? Whatever the reason, it didn't make him any easier to trust.

"Or something," Simon muttered.

"I think a female officer would have better luck getting this woman to confide in her," Jake said. "If we could persuade this woman to work with us, we could build a stronger case against the German."

On the outside, Carmen was Jane Cool, but inside she was groaning and covering her face with her hands. No one was going to believe that, were they?

"You're going to a lot of trouble to nail one plant collector," Simon said. "Why?"

"He may be only one man, but we suspect in the past year he's shipped over two thousand specimens, many of them rare and irreplaceable, out of the country," Jake said. "Some species have already been wiped out in the wild by similar collectors. My agency wants to send a strong message that this kind of destruction of resources won't be tolerated. In addition, if he can lead us to the dealers he supplies, we already have agreements in place with law enforcement in Europe that could enable us to shut down the market for these cactus."

"Officer Redhorse, do you have any objection to working with Agent Lohmiller?" Graham asked.

Yes, because the man tells the truth only when it's convenient, and he's too sexy for his own good, and I have a hard time keeping my mind solely on the job when he's around. She cleared her throat. "No, sir. It sounds like an interesting case."

"Officer Lohmiller, if you'll wait in the other room until we're done here, you can meet with Officer Redhorse," Graham said.

"Of course." He looked at Carmen at last. She hoped she was imagining the wink he gave her—and that no one else around the table had seen it.

The commander waited until the door had closed behind Jake, then returned to his seat at the head of the table. Carmen held her breath, hoping he wouldn't ask her if she had known about Jake and his cactus-smuggling case. She would have to admit the truth, and that would look very awkward.

"What were you saying before our interruption?" Graham asked.

She blinked. What had she been saying?

"Something else that happened while you were undercover in Metwater's camp," he prompted.

Right. She'd been about to tell them about Jake. But she couldn't do that now without looking guilty of something. Which she wasn't. She searched her mind for anything else plausible she could say and settled on the other curious thing she had made note of last night. "One of the women in camp, who goes by the name Starfall, has a big file of newspaper clippings about Daniel Metwater—not his writings as a prophet or anything like that, but articles about his life before he decided to wander in the wilderness. Quite a few of the articles are about his brother's death."

"The brother who was murdered," said the man next to Carmen, Marco Cruz with the DEA.

"Right," she said. "The police in Chicago suspected a hit by organized crime but weren't able to pin the murder on anyone."

"Why is this woman so interested?" Simon asked.

"I don't know," Carmen said. "But I thought it was odd. Something worth adding to the other information we have about Metwater and his group." And probably not worth bringing up, if she hadn't needed something to answer the commander's question.

"Be careful around the minnow Mountie," Simon said.

She stiffened at Simon's use of the slang term for a Fish and Wildlife officer. "Why do you say that?"

"I think it's suspicious that he didn't want to involve us until he needed help," Simon said. "And asking for a woman, when you were clearly the only woman in the room—I think he's up to something."

"Come on, Simon, would you want to work an undercover op with Lance, when you could have our resident beauty queen as your partner?" Marco asked.

Carmen tensed. Last month her mother had mailed a package to the office that included the crown and sash from her brief stint as Miss Southern Ute—a not-so-subtle reminder of Carmen's place in the tribe and part of an ongoing campaign by her parents to encourage her to leave the Ranger Brigade and sign on as a member of the Ute Tribal Police. She had made the mistake of opening the box in front of some of the guys, and now she might never hear the end of it. Carmen had even wondered if the teasing had been part of her mother's plan, too. Wilma Redhorse was a sharp attorney and a brilliant strategist, so Carmen wouldn't put it past her mom to foresee this development.

"Some people might consider that a sexist remark," Graham said.

Marco sent her an apologetic look. "No offense intended."

"I don't take offense," she said. "I take revenge."

"You're in trouble now," Lance said.

"I think we've said enough on the topic." Graham consulted the notebook in front of him. "Just a few updates on current cases to take care of…"

Carmen turned her attention back to the commander, but part of her mind was on the case ahead and the confounding, intriguing man she'd have to work with. Even though Jake made her uncomfortable, his case and its environmental and international implications interested her. This was the kind of case she had joined the Ranger Brigade to work on—something much bigger than keeping order on her family's reservation. Why couldn't her mother see that?

Half an hour later, Carmen stood with Jake in the parking lot behind Ranger headquarters, next to a battered and very dusty pickup truck, the bed piled with camping gear. "This definitely doesn't look like an official vehicle," she said.

"That's the idea."

She nodded toward the headquarters building. "Was all that really necessary in there? You couldn't have told the truth—that we met at Metwater's camp and you thought I could be useful to your case?"

"I wasn't sure you'd want your co-workers knowing we'd met before. After all, I'm the untrustworthy Cactus Cop."

His teasing tone almost made her smile—almost. But she wasn't about to let him think she was going soft. "I hope you don't really think I'm going to persuade Starfall to do anything for you—she hates my guts."

"I have faith in you."

"You don't need me to persuade her—make her think you've fallen for her charms, and she'd probably do anything for you."

"Then maybe you can make her think agreeing to help me is the best way to catch my attention."

"I'd be better off persuading her you're going to pay her a lot of money. The woman is seriously motivated by cash. When I was going through her trunk, searching for your badge, I came across a couple of things that made me wonder if she was holding other people's property hostage. Or blackmailing them." For instance, was there something in those articles she had collected about Daniel Metwater that she was using to blackmail the Prophet? She was the one woman in camp who didn't fawn over him, and yet she seemed to hold a position of privilege. It might be worth looking into…

"I'll leave it up to you to decide how best to approach Starfall." Jake brought her attention back to his investigation. "Whatever you can find out about her relationship with the German could be helpful, but I hope you'll also try to persuade my mom that she and Sophie need to leave Metwater's group—the sooner, the better."

"You left in a hurry yesterday afternoon," she

said. "And Phoenix wouldn't say anything when I asked if the two of you had had a nice visit."

"She told me that Daniel Metwater told her that he wants to marry Sophie!" His voice strained with agitation. "What kind of man says that about a fourteen-year-old?"

"Do you think she was telling the truth?" Carmen asked. "I mean, I'm not saying your mother is a liar, but that seems so preposterous."

"She said he intends to wait until Sophie is eighteen, but in the meantime she can prepare to be his *helpmate*." His look of disgust mirrored her own emotions. "I have to get her out of there," he said. "And I need to get Mom away from there, too, if I can. I stopped by to see her this morning, and she was still in bed—Sophie said she was resting, but when I saw her, she looked ill. They told me you'd left and showed me your note. That's when I decided to come to Ranger headquarters and plead my case."

"Did you really talk to your supervisor and ask him to bring me in?"

"Yes. I do sometimes tell the truth, you know. Most of the time, actually."

"All right. I'll talk to Starfall, but don't expect much. And I'll talk to Phoenix, too. If she really is ill, maybe I can persuade her to visit the clinic in town. And I'll try to find out more about this marriage proposition of Metwater's. If she still thinks I'm one of his followers, she might give me more details."

"That's what I'm hoping. When you talk to Starfall, make her think I really need her help."

"Or maybe I should tell her she shouldn't trust you as far as she can throw you."

The barb earned her a smile that sent heat curling through her. "You only say that in a feeble effort to resist my charms."

Flirting with him was too dangerous, so she focused on the job. "What are you going to do while I'm back in Metwater's camp?" she asked.

"I'm going to follow Werner Altbusser."

"Where is he right now?"

He checked his watch. "He told his waitress at breakfast this morning that he was going to spend the day at a local hot springs and spa. Apparently, smuggling endangered species is stressful, and he needed a break. I double-checked, and he had an appointment for a day full of treatments. Just in case he didn't show up or decided to leave early, I charmed the attendant at the spa into giving me a call. I told her he was my uncle, and I was planning a surprise party for him."

"And she believed you?"

"I can be very convincing."

She bet he could. One smoldering look from those blue eyes and a roguish smile, and the poor attendant had probably been weak at the knees. "Are you sure he's not just an ordinary tourist on vacation?" she asked, a little more sharply than she had intended.

"We've got video of him pocketing thousands of dollars' worth of rare cactus in four different states."

"Then why not arrest the guy now? Why go to all the trouble and expense of following him, when you already have plenty of evidence?"

"One count of plant theft doesn't carry much weight. The more evidence we can gather against him, the better chance we have of getting jail time and a really big fine—enough to make similar criminals take note and maybe think twice. And we still hope he can lead us to the really big fish—the dealers who purchase his finds."

"Carmen?"

She turned to see DEA agent Marco Cruz striding toward her. The muscular Latin officer wore a grim expression that immediately put her on alert. "What is it, Marco?"

He stopped in front of them. "We just had a report come in of a dead man in a tent over in the South Rim campground. He was reportedly shot in the back of the head."

"I guess a murder investigation trumps my plant case," Jake said.

"This might be part of your case," Marco said. "Supposedly, this guy had a whole backpack full of cactus in his vehicle."

Chapter Nine

Carmen stared down at the body of the young man she had known only as Reggae. He lay on his side a few feet off the trail, a faded, blue pack at his back.

"That's not my guy." Jake moved in behind her.

"No." He wasn't the German smuggler. He was just a kid who was searching for a place to belong. So why was he lying here dead?

"He doesn't have any ID on him." Marco said. He had brought Carmen and Jake here from Ranger headquarters. "Ethan thought he looked like the type who'd hang around Metwater."

"He was one of Metwater's followers," Carmen said. "He went by the name of Reggae." She squatted down for a closer look. His face in death looked very young and surprisingly peaceful. A small black hole above his right temple was the only sign of violence.

"A .22-caliber, close range." Marco crouched beside her and pointed to the wound. "You can see the powder burns."

"You said that pack is full of cactus?" Jake asked.

"Right." Marco stood. "No identification, no food or clothes or camping equipment, just an old garden trowel and about two dozen cactus plants."

"Mind if I take a look?" Jake asked.

"Go ahead." Marco glanced at Carmen. "Simon and Ethan processed the scene, since you were tied up with him." He jerked a thumb toward Jake, who was already kneeling beside the pack.

She nodded. As a member of the Colorado Bureau of Investigation, she usually took lead in processing crime scenes, but all the Rangers had the experience and training to handle the job. She turned to Jake. "Are those the cactus your collector is interested in?" she asked.

"Not the rare ones he asked Starfall to find for him. There are a few that might bring in a few bucks, but most of them are too common for Werner and his buyers to be interested in." He opened his palm to display a golf-ball sized round cactus, covered with hairy, pinkish spines. "If Werner hired this guy to gather specimens for him, he either didn't give him very good instructions, or Reggae ignored him."

"Maybe he wasn't working for Werner." Carmen stood also. "He was always hanging around Starfall, trying to impress her. Maybe he heard she was look- ing for cactus and thought gathering a bunch would be a good way to catch her attention." She glanced down at the dead man again and fought back a wave of sadness. Reggae had been trying to do something sweet for a woman he liked, and the gesture may have cost him his life.

"Any ideas who killed him, and why?" Marco asked.

"It wasn't Werner." Jake closed the pack and dusted off his hands. "He wouldn't want to call attention to himself, especially for a bunch of plants he couldn't use."

"A rival smuggler?" Marco asked.

Jake shook his head. "We haven't heard of anyone else operating in this area but, even if they were, why kill a dumb kid over plants you can't use?"

"Maybe it was a warning for Werner and his people to stay out of the rival group's territory," Carmen said.

Jake looked skeptical. "I'll check with my office, but I'm pretty sure we haven't heard of any other smugglers active in the cactus trade internationally. Werner and the few people he worked with have made a name for themselves with buyers."

"Maybe someone new is trying to take over the operation," Marco said. He looked down at the dead young man. "This doesn't have the feel of a random shooting. More like a deliberate hit."

"Do we have any witnesses?" Carmen asked. "Did anyone hear or see anything suspicious?"

"No one has come forward," Marco said. "The hiker who found the body called it in about two hours ago. The medical examiner estimates time of death at around five hours ago. He'll have a better estimate for us after the post mortem, but it rules out the guy who called it in. Five hours ago he was having breakfast in Montrose with three friends."

"Five hours ago would make it about seven a.m.," Jake said. "Werner was at his motel then. Somebody was out and about early."

"We'll have to talk to Metwater," Carmen said. "Try to find out Reggae's real name, and if he has any family."

"Metwater will swear he doesn't know anything," Marco said.

"We need to talk to Starfall, too," Jake said. "I want to know who she told about her cactus-selling sideline. And I want to find out if she knew what Reggae was up to."

"We'd better double-check where Werner was this morning," Carmen said. "In case he does have something to do with this."

"I'll stop by the spa and confirm his appointments," Jake said. He checked his watch. "I'll need to call my supervisor and report this latest development. Even if it's only coincidentally linked to my case, he'll want to know."

"We'll try to track down the people who signed the trail register this morning and question them," Marco said. "There are only three names, and one of them is the man who found the body."

"Who is he?" Jake asked.

"A geology professor from Ohio," Marco said. "He's completely freaked out about this."

"Maybe Reggae has an enemy we don't know anything about," Carmen said. "Someone from his past who tracked him down and decided to kill him."

"Let's hope Metwater or someone else in camp can tell us Reggae's real name, and we'll dig deeper into his background," Jake said.

"What should we do with the cactus?" Marco asked.

"Hold on to them as evidence until we're sure they have nothing to do with my case," Jake said.

"And if they don't?" Carmen asked.

He shrugged. "Usually we destroy them. Most of them wouldn't live if replanted. Cactus look hardy, but they're pretty difficult to transport and grow—another reason viable specimens are so valuable."

"So the murdered man collected the wrong type of cactus and ended up dead," Marco said. "Maybe because he made an enemy, and maybe because he was simply in the wrong place at the wrong time."

"Maybe the person who killed him was upset about the cactus theft itself," Carmen said. "A militant environmentalist."

"Those groups usually try to send a message and make a public statement," Marco said. "Killing one guy on a remote trail doesn't get them the kind of attention they want."

"It's worth checking into," Jake said. "But I agree, this doesn't fit that kind of scenario. To shoot a man up close, on a remote trail, feels personal."

"So we need to find out who wanted Reggae dead," she said. "And why."

"It could be because of something Reggae did," Jake said. "Or because the killer wanted to send a message to someone close to him."

"What kind of message?" she asked.

"I'd say when someone is killed, the message is almost always, *watch out—you could be next.*"

JAKE LEFT CARMEN with the crime-scene team and drove back to Montrose to check on Werner at the spa and to report in to his boss. He had agreed to pick Carmen up in a couple of hours on his way back to Metwater's camp.

Werner Altbusser was dozing under a mud mask, his rotund figure swathed in seaweed, when Jake looked in on him at the spa. The attendant reported he had been at the facility since eight that morning.

"I would have called if he left early," she said, her lips forming a pretty pout. "Don't you trust me?"

"This way I get to see you again." The words rolled off his tongue, but he felt guilty as soon as he said them. Flirting was second nature to him, especially when it netted information he wanted. But he could almost see Carmen frowning and shaking her head, dismissing him as shallow and manipulative. He shrugged off the image. He was doing his job, and who was she to judge him, anyway?

He called his supervisor, Resident Agent-in-Charge Ron Clark, from the parking lot of the spa and made his report. "I met with the Rangers, and they've assigned an agent to work with me on the local angle," Jake said. "Werner isn't collecting today—I get the impression he's waiting for something. Maybe he's expecting someone else to arrive—one of his fellow hobbyists." That was how the smugglers always characterized their activities, as an innocent hobby.

"Or he's lying low because he's worried about you." Agent Clark, a forty-year veteran who wore his cynicism as a badge of honor, had already lectured Jake about screwing up years of investigative work when he confronted Werner in his camp. Jake figured he was in for round two and braced himself for another tirade. But his boss kept his words brief. "We're pulling you off the case. We're sending another agent in this afternoon to take over the tail."

"I thought you said you didn't have anyone else to work the case," Jake said.

"A field agent from Grand Junction, Tony Davidson, has agreed to take over for the moment. You can return to Texas."

Being pulled from the case was bad, but being ordered back to Texas before he had had time to help his mother and Sophie was a disaster. "There's been another development that may be related to our case," Jake said. "A young man was murdered in the wilderness area where Werner was collecting yesterday. He had a backpack full of cactus. He may have been working for Werner."

"Why was he killed?" Clark barked the words.

"That's what we need to find out. I was going to head out this afternoon to question some people who knew the young man. He's a local, and part of the hippie group I was telling you about. He's a friend of the young woman Werner hired to collect for him, so it's possible Werner hired this young man, too. His killing could be the work of a rival smuggling group or a radical environmental group."

"Is that what the Rangers think? Are they aware of such groups operating in the area?"

"All they'll tell me is that they're considering a number of possibilities. You know how these other agencies are—very closemouthed. I think if we're going to learn anything useful, I really need to stay here as a part of their investigative team."

He held his breath, gripping the phone so tightly his fingers ached.

"All right." Clark sounded tired. "I can spare you for a few more days. Adding murder to the list of charges against Werner would lend some serious weight to our case."

"That's what I thought, sir." He didn't really think the German had anything to do with Reggae's death, but he would play up any possible link to gain more time to work on his mom. If he had to, he could turn her in to the local cops for violating Sophie's custody order, then he could take Sophie back to their grandparents. But he wanted to help his mom, not hurt her more. He wanted to persuade her and his sister to come with him willingly. She could get the medical help she needed, and the three of them could start rebuilding their family.

Also, he wasn't ready to leave Carmen Redhorse just yet. The strong, sexy sergeant had awakened something in him he had thought long dead—the desire to be with someone not just physically but also as a part of her life. He wanted more time to see where those feelings went and decide what he should do about them.

He picked her up at Ranger headquarters. As she slid into the front seat of his pickup, the intoxicating aromas of beef, onions and spices hit him, and his stomach growled. "Have some lunch," she said, handing him a foil-wrapped packet.

"What is it?" he asked, leaving the vehicle in Park and unwrapping the foil, inhaling the amazing scents.

"Indian taco." She unwrapped her own packet, then handed him a plastic fork. "You'll probably need this."

He took a forkful of the bean-and-meat mixture and all but moaned at the taste. "Did you make this?" he asked after he'd swallowed.

She shook her head. "My mom. She stopped by with enough for the whole office."

"If she does this regularly, you must be the most popular person on the team." He took another bite. "Amazing!"

"She's convinced I'll wither away without home

cooking. And she likes to remind me what I'm missing by not moving back home to the reservation."

"She really wants you to move home? And do what?"

"Work for the tribal police." She stirred the fork around her taco but didn't take another bite. "She thinks I should be using my education and training to help my people the way she and my dad did—she's a lawyer, and my dad has served on the tribal council."

"Sounds like a lot of pressure," he said.

She drank from a bottle of water and nodded. "My family has always had high expectations. When I was a kid, I didn't dare screw up. It wasn't allowed."

"My family had no expectations at all for me," he said. "It didn't matter what I did." Though in some ways that had felt freeing when he was younger, he had felt the lack of anyone rooting for—or even expecting him—to succeed.

"You seem to have done all right for yourself," she said. "Military veteran. Cop. Your mom should be really proud of you."

"I'm not so sure about that," he said. "Cops aren't her favorite people and, as a pacifist, she doesn't much approve of the military."

"So why did you go that route—army, then Fish and Wildlife?"

He had asked himself the same question more than once. "I think my life growing up was so chaotic that I gravitated toward organizations that were all about order." And that was enough of talking about himself. He turned the conversation back to her. "Do your parents expect you to marry someone from your tribe?" he asked.

"Oh, yes. Mom even has the man all picked out."

Her frown told him she didn't think much of the idea. "Seriously?" he asked. "Who's the lucky guy?"

"Rodney Tonaho. Tribal police chief. Former high-school basketball star, class valedictorian and all-around great guy."

"But not your guy?" He hoped he didn't sound too anxious about her answer to this question.

She slid her gaze over to him. "I prefer to pick my own men."

What were his chances of her picking him? She had kissed him last night at Metwater's camp, but that could have merely been curiosity or responding to the moment. She had made it pretty clear she didn't trust him. He had spent most of his life in situations that demanded he live by his wits. Sometimes that meant lying or pretending to be something he wasn't. He wasn't even sure he knew how to reveal his true self to another person.

He turned his attention away from such dangerous thoughts and focused once more on the food. "Thanks for sharing the bounty," he said. "I've never had an Indian taco before."

"Neither did the Utes, until they ended up on the reservation." She finished off the last of her lunch and crushed the foil into a ball. "We started making them to sell to tourists. They're tasty, but not something you'd want to eat every day—too much white flour and grease. If you want a real Native dish, you'll have to try some of my aunt Lucy's venison stew."

"Sounds good." He finished the last of his taco and wiped his hands on a napkin before putting the truck into gear. "Ready to reveal your true identity to Metwater and his followers?"

"I am," she said. "I'm looking forward to seeing the expression on Daniel Metwater's face when he finds out he was hosting a cop."

"You'd think a prophet would have seen through your disguise," Jake said.

"I'm sure he'll have an explanation for his followers." Her expression sobered. "Though I hope Sophie and your mom will understand why I kept the truth from them."

"My mom isn't going to be happy to find out I'm a cop, either." He glanced at her. "In her past, she had more than a few run-ins with the police, none of them pleasant." One of the toughest parts of his screening for his job had been admitting that his own mother had a record for drug possession, solicitation and theft. He might have had a tough time in some city police departments but, being a Fish and Wildlife officer, he rarely dealt with drug crimes and prostitution.

"Phoenix gives Daniel Metwater credit for getting her off drugs," Carmen said. "Whatever else he's done wrong, we have to applaud him for that."

"Yeah, good for him," Jake said. "But she needs to move on now. And she needs to let Sophie move on. Whether her story about Metwater wanting to marry Sophie is true or not, nothing good will come of the two of them staying with him."

"I agree," Carmen said. "And I'll do what I can to help you, though I don't see how I can have much influence."

"I want to talk to her first," he said. "Before we speak with Metwater and Starfall."

"Sure. It might even be good if they think she's the reason for our visit. It might cause them to let down their guard."

No one challenged them as they walked into camp from the parking area. "There's almost always a guard," Carmen said. "I wonder why no one is on duty today."

"Maybe it was Reggae's turn to keep watch," Jake said.

Almost everyone in the camp openly stared at them as they moved among the tents and trailers. Jake knew they were focusing on the uniforms more than the people in them—it was both a positive and a negative about the apparel. It marked officers as figures with special power, which some people respected, and most people feared, at least a little.

Starfall jumped up from the folding chair she had been sitting in by the door of the white tent and openly gaped at them, then ducked into the tent—

was she hiding or merely going to tell her tentmate, Asteria, about this latest development?

Sophie stared, too, when she opened the door of the trailer she shared with Phoenix. She took in Jake's dark brown pants and khaki uniform shirt, and the khaki pants and shirt Carmen wore, with her sergeant's stripes and blue Ranger Brigade patch. "Jake, why are you dressed like that?" she asked. "And Carmen—what's going on?"

"May we come in?" he asked. "You don't have to be afraid. You're not in any trouble."

She stepped back and let them move past her. Phoenix sat up from where she had been lying on the daybed and pushed a knitted afghan aside. She, too, stared at the uniforms. "Jake, please don't tell me you're a cop!" she all but wailed.

"I'm an investigator with the US Fish and Wildlife Service," he said. "My job is to protect our plant and animal resources."

His explanation did little to change the expression of disgust on her face. She turned to Carmen. "And you're one of those Rangers—the ones who are always hassling us. You weren't here as our friend at all. You were spying on us."

"I was trying to learn more about the group," she said. "Trying to understand you."

"And to think I thought of you as my friend." She looked away. "You can both leave now."

"We're not leaving," Jake said. "We're both here because we care about the two of you." He sat beside

Phoenix and took her hand. "Mom, you're clearly not well. Look at you—having to lie down in the middle of the day. That isn't like you."

"I'm not as young as I used to be." She pushed her limp hair back off her forehead. "I've been taking a tonic I'm sure will help me, but herbal medicines take a while to work."

"What are your symptoms?" Carmen asked. "And what are you taking for them?"

"I'm taking molasses and apple cider vinegar to strengthen my blood, and dandelion root for fatigue," Phoenix said. "It's all very healthy, nothing narcotic or illegal."

"You need to see a doctor, to make sure it isn't something more serious," Jake said. "There's a clinic in town. I could take you."

"You won't bring me back here," she said. "You hate the Prophet—you're afraid of his power." She turned to Carmen. "He told me that's why the Rangers are always bothering us—they know that the Prophet is more powerful than they are, that if everyone followed the peaceful way he preaches, it would put them out of work."

Jake saw that this twisted logic made perfect sense to her, but Sophie wasn't buying it. "Some people don't want to be peaceful," she said. "Jake and Carmen will always have work trying to protect the rest of us from them." She touched his shoulder. "Why are you here today?"

"We have some sad news," he said. "One of your

members, a man named Reggae, was killed early this morning. It may be related to a case I'm working on."

Sophie's eyes widened. "Reggae?"

He took both her hands in his. "Yes, but you can't say anything to anyone until we've told Metwater. We're hoping he can tell us how to get in touch with Reggae's family."

She nodded, her eyes bright with tears. "He was always nice to me," she said. "I'm sorry he's dead."

"What kind of case?" Phoenix asked.

"An illegal smuggling operation." He squeezed her hand. "I can't say more."

"And you think the Prophet had something to do with this?" Phoenix looked indignant. "Well, you're wrong."

"We don't have any reason to believe he's involved," Carmen said. "Why do you think we would?"

"Have there been any strangers in camp lately?" Jake asked. "People with foreign accents?"

"Don't be ridiculous." She folded her arms across her chest and looked away again.

Jake turned to his sister. "Have you seen or heard anything unusual in the past few days?"

She shook her head. "No. No one has visited— just you and Carmen. What kind of foreign accent?"

"It doesn't matter." He stood. "We'd better go see Metwater now."

"You can walk with us to his motor home," Carmen said to Sophie. "If it's okay with your mother."

"I'll go with you," Sophie said, jumping up and running out before her mother could object.

"The clinic in town is very good," Carmen said to Phoenix. "The nurse practitioner is a friend of mine, and the fees are on a sliding scale."

Phoenix said nothing and kept her gaze fixed out the window. As soon as they were out of the trailer, Jake put his arm around his sister and pulled her close. "How are you doing?" he asked.

"Okay." She shrugged. "I'm worried about Mom."

"She doesn't look very well," Carmen said. "Is she eating?"

"Not much." Sophie shook her head. "She said everything upsets her stomach. She sleeps a lot. The Prophet excused her from work duties." She looked up at Jake. "He even tried to get her to see the doctor. He's not all bad."

"I'm glad to hear it," Jake said. "Try not to worry too much. That's my job."

"I can't believe you're a cop," Sophie said. "Mom hates cops." She flushed. "Only because she got in so much trouble with them when she was doing drugs and stuff."

"Your mom isn't in any trouble with us," Carmen said. "We only want to help."

"I know," Sophie said.

They reached Metwater's motor home. "Go back to Mom," Jake said. "I'll try to check in with you again tomorrow, but, if you need anything at all, here's my number." He took one of his cards from his shirt pocket and handed it to her.

She studied the card. "We don't have a phone. No one does. They don't work out here."

"Get someone to bring you to Ranger head-quarters," Carmen said. "You can call from there, or I'll help you."

She nodded and slipped the card into the pocket of her jeans. "I guess being a wildlife officer is a good job, huh?" she asked.

"I think so."

"Good enough to support all of us if we came to live with you?"

"Definitely good enough for that."

She hugged him, then hurried away, back toward Phoenix's trailer. Jake and Carmen climbed the steps of Metwater's RV. The door opened before Jake could knock. Asteria looked out at them. "The Prophet wants to know why you're here," she said.

"We came to inform him of the death of one of his followers," Jake said.

She looked startled but said nothing and held the door open wider for them to enter. Metwater sat in a recliner across the room, feet up, posture relaxed. He, too, remained silent as they entered, though Jake could read the contempt in his expression from across the room.

"One of your followers, Reggae, is dead," Jake said. "We need to know his real name so that we can contact his family."

"I wondered where he was this morning," Metwater said. "It wasn't like him to shirk his duties."

"Aren't you curious as to how he died?" Jake asked.

"I assume you'll tell me."

"He was murdered," Jake said.

Still, Metwater's expression betrayed nothing. It was the face of a statue—handsome and unfeeling. He turned to Carmen. "Why are you here?"

"I knew Reggae," she said. "I came to tell his friends what happened to him and to find out what I could about him—to try to find the person who killed him."

"And you think it was one of us, don't you? That's what the Rangers always think." He shifted position, bringing the recliner upright with a thump. "Get out of my house. I welcomed you in because I thought you were a believer, yet it was all lies. You came here as a spy and my enemy. Get out."

Carmen didn't flinch, though Jake sensed her tension. He wasn't sure he could have withstood Metwater's raging without firing back, but she kept calm. "I have a job to do," she said. "One that includes protecting all the people in this camp—and you. Do you know anyone who would have any reason to execute Reggae with a bullet to his temple?"

Metwater's face had been flushed with rage, but now it was drained of color. "Why did you use that word—*executed*?"

"Because that is what Reggae's death reminded

me of," she said. "He was shot in the temple with a small-caliber weapon, the gun so close there were powder burns. His hands were tied behind his back. We can't be certain, but my guess would be more than one person was involved. They probably made him kneel in the dirt and killed him there."

Metwater looked ill. Asteria moved over to put a hand on his shoulder. "You should go," she told Jake and Carmen. "The Prophet is deeply affected by violence. It's because he's a man of peace."

"That's not the reason, is it?" Jake asked. Metwater hadn't reacted at all to news of Reggae's death, only to the specific manner of that death.

Metwater shook his head. "Go," he said, the single syllable a croak. "Just…go."

They left. Outside the motor home, Jake turned to Carmen. "What do you make of that?"

"He looked terrified," she said.

"Like someone who got a message he didn't want to receive," Jake said. "Let's see if anyone else in camp can shed any light."

"Starfall," Carmen said. "She has a whole file on the Prophet. Almost like a dossier. I found it when I was searching for your badge."

Starfall had returned to the folding chair outside her tent. "I knew there was a reason you two were so cozy," she said as they approached. "You're just a pair of pigs."

"I thought that slang went out of fashion years ago," Jake said.

"We're a little behind the times here," Starfall said. "Haven't you noticed?"

"I'm afraid we have some bad news," Jake said.

"The only bad news is that you two are here," Starfall said.

"Reggae is dead," Carmen said. "Someone killed him this morning."

Starfall stared. "No."

"I'm sorry, yes." Carmen squatted down in front of her chair. "We're trying to find out who killed him. Did he ever mention any enemies to you? Anyone who might want to harm him?"

Starfall shook her head. "Not Reggae. He was a nice guy." She blinked, her eyes shiny. "A really nice guy."

"This wasn't an accident," Jake said. "He had a backpack full of cactus. Was he collecting them for you?"

"For me?" She swallowed. "I told him a guy would pay for cactus, but that was all. He never said anything about wanting to get in on the deal."

"Maybe he wanted to surprise you," Jake said.

"That would be just like him." She gave a ragged laugh. "He was always trying to impress me. If I said I wanted wild strawberries, he'd pick a big bowl full. Or if we needed something repaired, he would always volunteer." She swallowed, tears streaming down her cheeks. "I was pretty awful to him, really, and he was so nice to me."

"I'm sorry," Carmen said. "I know he was your friend."

"How did he die?" Starfall said. "I mean, you said he was shot, but how?"

"A bullet in his temple," Carmen said.

"You mean, like an execution—like a mob hit or something?"

"Why do you say *mob*?" Jake said.

Starfall shook her head, as if trying to clear it. "It's just funny, that's all."

"What's funny?" Carmen asked.

"For him to die that way." Her eyes, without their usual guile, met Jake's. "That's the same way Daniel Metwater's brother was killed."

Chapter Ten

A search of Reggae's tent revealed that his real name was Donald Quackenbush, from Pocatello, Idaho. He had no criminal record, and the only family the Rangers could locate was an older sister who reported she hadn't seen her brother in five years and didn't have the time or money to come get him now.

Carmen hung up the phone from that conversation feeling a too-familiar mixture of anger and disgust. At least Starfall had truly grieved the young man's death, and Daniel Metwater had sent word half an hour ago that he would pay for Reggae's cremation if the ashes were returned to the Family, so that they could give him a formal memorial.

"The sister says she has no idea what her brother has been doing all these years," Carmen told Jake. He had pulled up a chair to the opposite side of her desk and was sharing the workspace with her. On the way back from Metwater's camp, he had revealed that he was no longer assigned to tail Werner Altbusser but would work with the Rangers on the murder investigation.

"I found a couple of articles about David Metwater's death," he said, looking up from his laptop. "Starfall is right—he was shot in the right temple with a .22-caliber pistol. His hands were tied behind him, and he was dumped in the river."

"It could be a coincidence," Carmen said. "Or maybe the mob is branching out into cactus smuggling."

"Or maybe someone is sending a message to Daniel Metwater, and Donald was the unfortunate means of delivering the message."

"Metwater was certainly affected by the news," Carmen said. "I can see how it would be a shock to hear about someone else he knew dying the same way as his brother, even if Reggae's murder has nothing to do with Metwater."

"I'm having a hard time seeing a connection," Jake said. "David Metwater died almost two years ago. Daniel Metwater hasn't made any big secret of his whereabouts or what he's been doing. Why would the mob decide all of a sudden to come after him?"

She ran both hands through her hair. "I don't know. And I'm too beat to come up with any good theories tonight. Let's pack it in until tomorrow."

"Good idea." He powered down his laptop. "Want to grab a bite to eat?" he asked. "You provided lunch—it's only fair I should buy you dinner."

She should say no. Getting involved with a coworker was a bad idea, even if he was only temporarily liaising with the Rangers. And part of her still wasn't sure she could trust him. "Okay," she said. They would talk about work, she promised herself. Two co-workers reviewing the day.

She directed him to a café in town with good soups and salads and a choice of entrées that included, but wasn't limited to, burgers. "I like this town," Jake said as he settled into a booth across from her. "I wish I had more time to stick around and explore the area."

"It's a lot different from Houston," she said. "I was there once, visiting cousins. I remember heat, humidity and very flat terrain."

"It's great if you like big cities," he said. "But I'm thinking I should move Sophie and Mom someplace quieter. Maybe where Mom won't have so many temptations to slip back into her old life."

The mention of Phoenix sobered Carmen. "She doesn't look well," she said. "Even Metwater noticed. Maybe we can persuade him to order her to see a doctor. She might listen to him."

"I'm willing to try anything at this point." He set aside his menu. He looked beat—fatigue in his eyes and weariness in the set of his shoulders. She had to resist the urge to lean over the table and squeeze his hand.

Instead, she searched for a safe topic of conversation. "What's going to happen with Werner?" she asked.

"The other agent will tail him and get the photographs we need for our case. I met the agent—Tony—a couple of times at training seminars. He seems like a good guy—he'll do a good job."

"And you? Is this a setback for you?" His supervisor couldn't have been happy about Jake making contact with their suspect.

"It depends on what else I can turn up. We know Werner isn't working alone. He has partners overseas, and we suspect here in the States also. People who cover for him and maybe do some collecting for him."

"Maybe one of them got into an argument with Reggae. Maybe we're looking at this wrong, and he didn't collect those cactus—he took them from someone else."

"Except the cactus in that pack were worthless," Jake said. "And the way Reggae was killed wasn't an argument gone south."

"Right." The waitress took their orders—Thai chicken salad for her and blackened trout for him.

"I don't understand how the smugglers get enough rare cactus to make it worth their while," she said when they were alone again. "There are millions of acres of public land, but they can't possibly search every inch of that space for a type of cactus that may only be a few inches across."

"No, they can't. They have to have help. They can study terrain through things like Google Earth and isolate the most likely habitat. Sometimes they contact private landowners and ask permission to collect on their land. Most people don't realize it's illegal. Some of them see it as a good thing, getting rid of a nuisance."

"Or maybe sometimes they trespass," she said. "That happens on tribal land all the time. People think it's just empty land, so it's okay for them to camp or hunt arrowheads or whatever. The tribal council has spent a lot of money on fences and signs and efforts to educate the public."

"I envy you," he said. "Being part of a cohesive group like that. I imagine it's like an extended family. That's something I don't have. Maybe that's why Metwater's bunch appealed to my mom. She wanted that sense of belonging."

"A tribe is a family," she said. "It's a connection to a people and a heritage, and also to land where my family has lived for generations."

Jake sat back in the booth, studying her. "How did you get into law enforcement?" he asked.

"I was going to be a teen counselor," she said. "To pay for my schooling, I took a job at a youth detention center. Talking with the officers who worked there got me interested in law enforcement. I went through the police academy and decided I wanted to focus on investigations. I went back to school for more training, got on with CBI, then, when the federal government decided to form the Ranger Brigade to police public land, I applied and was accepted." She shrugged. "I like being closer to home."

"But not too close," he said. "Otherwise, you'd take the job with the tribal police."

"Right." She traced a bead of condensation down the side of her iced-tea glass. "I love my parents, but I need space to live my own life. They have this whole plan for my life, but I need to figure out my own direction. It's like—no matter what I do, they think I could do better."

"That kind of pressure would make some people give up," he said. "Seems to me you've done the opposite and worked hard to excel."

"Yes, I have." But sometimes she wondered if all her striving had been worth the cost. She had focused so much on being the best in an arena dominated by men that she hadn't even had one serious relationship, at an age when so many of the girls she had gone to school with were married with children. If she had bent to her parents' wishes and returned to reservation life, would she, too, be married with babies of her own?

The server brought their meals, and they ate in silence for a while. What Jake had said earlier about the smugglers taking advantage, coupled with her own stories about reservation life, had planted an idea in her head. "Would you like to come with me to the reservation tomorrow?" she asked.

He paused with his fork halfway to his lips and stared at her. "You're inviting me to your reservation?"

"There are a couple of people I want to talk to,"

she said. "They might be able to help us with this case."

"How?" he asked.

"It's complicated. And it may lead nowhere." She stabbed at a chunk of lettuce. "We don't have to go. It was just an idea."

"No. I'd love to come with you." He grinned. "I want to meet your parents. I promise to be on my best behavior."

JAKE FELT LIKE a guilty man facing cross-examination by a prosecutor who had never lost a case as he sat across the desk from Wilma Redhorse in her offices in the Southern Ute Tribal Council Center. The glass and concrete high-rise was not the reservation architecture he had expected, but the briefest tour of the Southern Ute Reservation near Ignacio, Colorado, showed him that his ideas about reservation life, at least for this tribe, were sadly outdated. In addition to the building that housed the tribal council, there was a high-rise hotel and casino, expansive cultural center and museum, business center, fitness center and more.

"Carmen tells me you two are working on a case together," Wilma Redhorse said. She was a slightly older version of her daughter, her black hair hanging loose about the shoulders of her stylish red business suit, black eyes piercing behind chic square-framed glasses. "But you're not a member of the Ranger Brigade."

"No ma'am. I'm conducting an investigation for Fish and Wildlife, and the Rangers have a case that may be related to mine. It made sense to work together." He wished he had listened to his instincts and worn his uniform. The brown and khaki combination gave him authority and identified him as one of the good guys. Instead, at Carmen's request, he had dressed in jeans and a western shirt and boots. She also wore jeans and a sleeveless blouse that showed off her toned upper arms. Of course, she had no need for an identifying uniform here— everyone already knew her and everything about her.

"Where are you from originally?" Mrs. Redhorse asked. "Where is your family?"

"We moved around a lot when I was a kid," he said. "Right now, I live in Houston, but my mother and younger sister are in Montrose County."

"No family in Houston?"

"No, ma'am." He sensed his lack of kin made him lesser in her eyes, but that might have been his own self-consciousness putting thoughts into his head. "I'm trying to persuade my mother and sister to come live with me," he added.

She nodded. "Families should be together, but not everyone sees it that way." She looked over his shoulder at her daughter when she spoke.

"Mom, what about the cactus collectors I asked you about?" Carmen asked, her voice crisp and business-like. "Has anyone like that asked to collect on tribal land or been caught trespassing?"

"If they have, I haven't heard of it," Wilma said. "They haven't asked permission and, if they had, it wouldn't have been granted." She turned to Jake. "We're trying very hard to preserve all our resources. The only reason we have this land is that the government thought it was useless. When oil and gas were discovered here, the mineral rights provided opportunities for our people. If we have valuable cactus, we'll decide what to do with it, not a bunch of European collectors."

"Would anyone else know if someone had asked about cactus?" Carmen asked.

"You should talk to Chief Tonaho. If anyone was caught trespassing or trying to dig up any cactus, he would know. And he would like to see you. He always asks me when you are going to come work for him."

"I like the job I have," Carmen said, with the weary tone of someone who has given the same answer many times but knows the words aren't really heard.

Wilma's gaze shifted to Jake. "The tribal police chief and Carmen grew up together. He knows how smart she is. He could use someone like her helping him. I always tell her they would make a great team."

"I'm certainly happy to have her as my partner," he said. Let her mom make of that remark what she would. Not that he and Carmen were partners in anything but a professional sense, but it wouldn't hurt to keep Wilma guessing.

"We'll go talk to Rodney," Carmen said. "I'd like him to meet Jake. Then we'll stop and talk to Aunt Connie."

Wilma frowned. "You're not sick, are you?" She leaned closer to study her daughter. "You look tired."

"I'm fine. We only want to ask Aunt Connie's opinion on something."

"What do you need an opinion on?" Wilma asked.

"I have a medical question for her," Carmen said. "Nothing to do with me, I promise." She moved to the door. "Come on, Jake."

He stood. "It was nice meeting you, Mrs. Red-horse," he said.

She nodded. "Good luck with your case, Agent Lohmiller."

Jake let out a breath as the door to the office closed behind him. "Notice she didn't say it was nice to meet me," he said.

"Hurry," she said as they walked back to her car, a gray Camry she had insisted on driving instead of his filthy pickup. "She'll call Rodney and tell him we're coming. Later, she'll call him and Connie before we're even off the reservation and find out everything she said to us."

"I'm a little jealous," he said.

"Of Rodney? Don't be. He's a nice guy, but not my type."

Some time he might ask her what her type was, but he didn't want to derail the conversation. "I can see how your mother's concern could be a bit oppressive, but my mom has always been so involved in her own problems that half the time she had no idea where I was or anything that was going on in my life."

Carmen looked over the top of the Camry at him. "Your mother loves you," she said. "I'll never forget the look on her face when you walked into Metwater's RV that first day and she realized it was you."

"I know she loves me," he said, opening the passenger side door of the car. "I'm just pointing out that having a parent who is concerned about you and the choices you make isn't all a bad thing."

She nodded and ducked into the driver's seat. "You're right. I know my mom wants the best for me, I just wish we were on the same page more often about what that is."

She started the car and turned left out of the parking lot. "Tell me about Rodney Tonaho," he said. "What should I expect?"

"Aside from being a high-school basketball star and the class valedictorian, he won every award there was, went off to college and it was pretty much a repeat performance. He's the youngest police chief we've ever had."

"No wonder your mother loves him."

"Everyone loves Rodney," she said. "He's very charming."

"Charm is overrated."

She laughed. The sound relaxed him a little. At least she hadn't fallen under Mr. Perfect's spell.

Rodney Tonaho greeted them at the door of his office. "It's good to see you again," he said, shaking Carmen's hand. "Your mother called and said you were coming." He turned and offered his hand to Jake. "You must be Agent Lohmiller."

The handshake was firm but not painful. Perfect, like everything else about the man, from his starched and pressed uniform to his movie-star good looks. Jake reminded himself that just because the man had apparently never had to struggle for anything in his life didn't mean he wasn't a nice guy and a good law enforcement officer. But he was going to have to prove himself before Jake would trust him.

"We're investigating a case that involves smuggling rare cactus," Carmen said when she and Jake were seated across from Rodney's desk in his office.

Rodney steepled his fingers and nodded. "So Wilma said. I don't know of anything like that going on on the reservation."

"The guy I'm tracking is a German named Werner Altbusser," Jake said. "He, or someone representing him, might contact you about collecting cactus on tribal land. Or they might simply trespass and dig up what they want without permission."

Rodney scowled, which only made him more rugged and handsome. "If they try that, they won't get away with it. We view trespassing and theft very seriously."

"Let us know if anything like that happens," Carmen said. "And be careful. One man who may have been working for Werner has already been murdered."

Rodney's expression relaxed. "Of course I'll let you know if anything comes up."

"Thanks." She stood. "We won't take up any more of your time."

"I'm always happy to see you," he said.

Jake heard the truth behind his words, and glimpsed the longing in Rodney's eyes that set off alarm bells in his head. His hands tightened on the arm of his chair as he stared at the man across the desk. Carmen might think the chief wasn't her type, but Rodney definitely had feelings for her.

"It was a long shot, but I thought it was worth checking out," she said as they set out in her car again.

"It was a good idea," Jake said. "Will he really call if he hears anything?"

She glanced at him. "Of course he will. Why wouldn't he?"

He shrugged. "I don't know. He would want to help you, but maybe not me?"

"Why wouldn't he want to help you?"

"He might see me as a rival for your affections."

She slammed on the brakes, throwing him forward, then pulled to the side of the road and stopped the car. "What are you talking about?" she asked.

He forced himself not to squirm in his seat. "I like you," he said. "I'm attracted to you. And I'm guessing by the way you kissed me the other night that you're attracted to me, too."

She looked away, but he didn't miss the flush that warmed her cheeks. "It was just a kiss," she said. "We work together."

And people who worked together sometimes got involved. That was life. But if she wanted to play that game, he could, too. "Fine. Forget I mentioned it. Tell me why we're going to see your aunt." he asked.

"She's a nurse practitioner at the tribal clinic." She glanced at him. "I wanted to ask her about your mom, if that's okay with you."

So much for keeping things strictly business. He couldn't explain why her concern for his mom moved him so—maybe because, on some level, it felt like she was caring about him, too. "That would be great," he said. "I'd love to get a professional's opinion."

Connie Owl Woman was a short, round woman who wore her silver hair in a long braid coiled at the back of her head. Her blue eyeshadow matched her blue scrubs, and she squealed with delight and gathered her niece in a crushing hug when Carmen and Jake walked into her office at the clinic. "Your mother already called and told me you were on your way over," she said. "And you must be Jake." She pumped his hand, her fingers squeezing all the feeling out of his. "Wilma said you and Carmen are working together."

"It's good to meet you," Jake said, reclaiming his hand and flexing his aching fingers.

"What can I do for you two today?" Connie beamed at them. "You both look healthy enough to me."

"We wanted to ask you about Jake's mother," Carmen said. "She's been ill."

Connie's face sobered. "What kind of illness?"

"I don't know," Jake said. "She refuses to see a doctor. She's very pale and tires easily. She's fainted a few times, and she says nothing agrees with her when she eats."

"Any history of health problems?"

"Not really." Jake hesitated, then added, "She has a history of drug use. She was addicted to heroin, though she's been clean for a while."

"Hepatitis is always a risk with a history of drug use," Connie said. "But what you're describing could be almost anything—anemia or something more serious—even cancer." She shook her head. "Impossible to tell without an examination and probably some blood work."

"That's what I was afraid you'd say," Jake said. "She's very stubborn about seeing a doctor, thinks she can cure herself with herbal remedies."

"There are some excellent herbal remedies out there," Connie said. "I have patients who rely on them. But there are times when modern medicine is just the thing." She patted his arm. "Your mother is probably afraid. I see it all the time. Especially if the sick person believes the disease is somehow their own fault. Your mother may believe her past behaviors led to her current illness, and she has the attitude she's only getting what she deserves, and she deserves to suffer. Which is ridiculous, but people believe ridiculous things every day. Some of us are more prone to it than others."

"Do you have any advice for getting her to see a doctor?" Jake asked.

She shook her head. "You might remind her that knowledge gives her power. Finding out what is going on with her health will give her the information she needs to make the right decisions. Sometimes framing it as a way of gaining control, when the person is afraid of having control taken away, can help."

"I'll try that. Thank you."

Connie reached over and patted Carmen's shoulder. "It is good to see you," she said. "You should come back for the powwow next month. Bring your friend here with you. Stay the weekend so he can get to know everyone."

Carmen smoothed back her hair and avoided looking at Jake. "I imagine he'll be back in Houston by then."

Connie shook her head. "Oh, I don't think so." She patted Jake's shoulder now. "Come back next month."

"Maybe I will."

They left the clinic, and he waited until they were in the car again before he spoke. "Why doesn't your

aunt think I'll be in Houston by next month—and
why do you think I will be?"

"You're here on temporary assignment," she said.
"You're from Houston. When the case is over, you'll
go back." She gripped the steering wheel with both
hands but didn't turn the key in the ignition.

"I need to settle my mother and sister in a place
that's good for them," he said. "I already told you
I don't think a big city like Houston is that place.
Maybe this is."

"What about your job?"

"There are other jobs. I could transfer or work
somewhere else. I'm used to going where the next
opportunity takes me."

She didn't relax her grip on the wheel. "I can't
imagine living like that," she said. "I've always had
a plan for my life—a next step to get where I want
to go."

"If that works for you, that's great," he said. "It
never worked for me." Life was full of too many
variables. If his mom didn't pay the rent, they might
have to leave in the middle of the night and find a
new apartment across town, or in another town altogether. If she ended up in jail, Jake had to drop
everything and look after Sophie. If he missed work
to babysit his sister while his mother was roaming
the streets in search of drugs, he might lose his job
and have to find another one. All that uncertainty
had taught him how to think on his feet. It had taught
him not to rely on other people. Maybe to someone

like Carmen, it made him seem unreliable. Someone she couldn't trust.

She dropped her hands to her lap and sighed. "Aunt Connie likes to make predictions about people," she said. "She says she's a good judge of character."

"Is she? Do her predictions come true?"

She shrugged. "Sometimes." She shifted the car into gear and flipped on her blinker before turning onto the road. "She liked you, so that's something in your favor."

"I liked her, too."

She pulled the car back onto the highway. "Do you want to see where I grew up?" she asked.

The question surprised him. The offer felt somehow intimate. Another acknowledgment that maybe not everything between them was strictly professional. "Yes, I'd like that."

She nodded and turned the car away from the clinic and the casino and office buildings toward country that quickly grew more rural—housing developments and shopping strips gave way to hayfields and pasture. She turned onto a gravel lane that led through an open iron gate, past white-fenced paddocks and a towering red barn. "My father raises cutting horses," she said. "Some of his horses are champions. It's his passion."

The drive curved past more paddocks and a modest white ranch house. "Home, sweet home," she said, slowing in front of the house. "I'd take you in and introduce you, but my father is at a sale over in Farmington today."

"It looks like a good place to grow up." He glanced at her. "Were you happy?"

"Yes. Even though I don't want to live here right now, I love having this place to come back to. I never understood Metwater's followers wanting to come together to make a kind of fake tribe," she said. "I didn't think it could possibly be anything like the real tribe I was a part of. But then, when I went to live with them for a few days and really got to know them, I realized they were searching for what I had already found. Their makeshift family might be a substitute for the real thing, but it was better than whatever they had had before. I saw the strength in what they were trying to do—the courage it took to trust others enough to build something that had been handed to me for nothing and with no effort on my part. It made me a little more compassionate, I think."

"My mother has a real family," he said. "Me, my sister, and her parents and brothers and sisters. She's hurt them, but I believe they still love her. I want us to try to be a family again. That would be better for Sophie than any fake family led by a pretend prophet."

"I hope your mom will give them a chance," Carmen said. She turned toward him. "What do you want to do now?"

He wanted to prolong the time with her and see

more of this personal side of her. Driving through this ranch, he could imagine her as a girl, riding a horse across the pasture, her long hair streaming behind her. "Show me your favorite place on the ranch," he said.

She hesitated, then nodded. "All right."

She drove past the ranch house and turned down a road that was little more than two ruts winding up a steep hill. At the top, she parked the car beside a stack of boulders and got out. Jake followed her to a twisted pine, where the land fell away in a steep cliff, the valley below a patchwork of plowed fields, pastures and homes. "When I was growing up, this was my whole world," she said. "This was my kingdom, and I was the queen."

He put his arm around her, and she leaned in to him. "I could see you as queen," he said. "You've got the attitude and the courage."

"Some men have a problem with the attitude," she said. "They say they admire strong women, but they don't want to be with them."

"I'm not one of those men." He turned her toward him, so that they stood face to face, hip to hip. "Why did you bring me here?" he asked.

"Because you asked. And because I wanted to do this." She cupped his face in her hands and pulled his mouth down to hers, the kiss as strong and confident as the woman, a meeting of their lips that was as much mental as physical. He lost focus on anything else as he wrapped both arms around her and pulled her close. He flashed back to the first day he had seen her, striding across the prairie, beautiful and wary as a wild horse. Holding her now, he still felt that wildness, an energy beneath his touch that reminded him she was allowing him to be with her this way but might change her mind at any moment.

She pulled slightly away, and he looked down into her eyes, trying to read the emotions there. "That wasn't just a kiss," he said and smoothed the pad of his thumb over her bottom lip.

"No," she said and moved closer, fitting her body between his legs, the soft fullness of her breasts pressed against his rib cage. He grasped her hips, splaying his fingers along their curves, letting her feel how much he wanted her. If she was going to run, now would be the time.

But instead of running, she pulled him down onto the soft bed of pine needles beneath the tree. He rolled onto his back, bringing her on top of him. She looked down on him and brushed the hair back from his eyes. "When I met you that first day near the camp, I was a little bit afraid of you," she said. "I still am."

He stroked her arm, a gentling motion. "You don't have to be afraid of me."

"Then maybe I'm more afraid of myself and what I might do with you."

"I can think of a few things I'd like to do right now." He stared into her eyes, losing himself in those brown depths, letting himself be that vulnerable. "One thing."

"I suddenly can't think of anything else." She kissed him again, a long, drugging kiss of tangled tongues and tangled limbs, her fingers moving along with her mouth, unbuttoning his shirt, her touch sending hot tendrils of sensation through him to pool in his groin.

"Are you sure this is what you want?" He made himself ask the question, though there was only one answer he wanted to hear.

"Oh, yes." She kissed his neck, then stroked her tongue across his pounding pulse. "This is exactly what I want."

They didn't talk much after that. Words seemed useless compared to the messages their bodies telegraphed. Though he would have kept some of his clothes on in deference to their exposed position, she insisted on removing every stitch, and he had to admit the sight of the sun gleaming on her body was one he would always treasure. When she took a condom from the pocket of her jeans, he laughed out loud. "So you were planning to bring me up here and seduce me," he said.

"Not planning, exactly." She held the packet up to him. "You might have said no."

"But you knew I wouldn't." He knelt in front of her and ripped open the packet. "You knew I couldn't." He sheathed himself, then lay back once more, pulling her on top of him. She held herself above him for a long moment, staring into his eyes, as if searching for something there. He didn't look away, trying to let her know without words how much she was coming to mean to him. Then he lost focus as she lowered herself over him and began to rock her hips gently, and then with more force, driving them both to a place he had been wanting to go since the moment he met her.

WHEN JAKE OFFERED to drive back to Montrose, Carmen let him. She didn't often surrender the wheel to someone else, but considering how much she had given to him already that day, driving seemed a small thing. She wanted time to think, without the distraction of steep mountain passes and narrow, winding switchbacks.

The man beside her was distraction enough. She could still feel the tension of his muscles beneath his fingers, the strength of him as he lifted her up with each thrust of his pelvis. Making love to him in the open like that, she had felt so vulnerable and at the same time so powerful. She had never done anything so daring with anyone before—had never wanted to even. But Jake made her want to be daring, almost as if she was trying to prove something to him, or to herself. *Look how bold I can be! Look at the risks I'll take!*

But being with him felt like the biggest risk of all. He was so many things she had decided would make the absolutely wrong partner for her. First of all, he was a cop—a man with a dangerous job and lousy hours and a world view that required him to regard everyone with suspicion. Just because she understood what that was like didn't mean she wanted to live with it every day, no matter what her mother predicted.

Then there was his family. He didn't have an ex-wife or a kid, other *no-no*s on her list, but he had a teenage sister and a mother who needed looking after. She liked Sophie, and she liked Phoenix, too, but relationships were tough enough without those kinds of personal complications.

Jake was good at his job, willing to do what was necessary to conduct an investigation, even if it meant pretending to be someone else. She approached her job with the same kind of determination but, if a man was so very good at lying on the job, how could she trust him not to lie to her in real life? And would she be tempted to lie to him? Wouldn't it be better to avoid putting themselves in a position where they would have to find out?

Safer, maybe. But that wasn't the same as better. With the scent of him still on her and the memory of his touch still tantalizing her nerve endings, she couldn't think of anything but how intoxicating being with him was—like a dangerous drug she could all too easily become addicted to.

Her phone beeped as they crossed the last pass. "We must be back in range of cell service," Jake said, pulling out his cell. "I've got a call."

"Me, too."

He pulled to the side of the road. "I'd better check this," he said.

She took out her own phone and called up voice mail. Marco Cruz's message was clipped and to the point. "You need to get back to Ranger headquarters," he said. "Daniel Metwater is here, and he's asking for you."

Chapter Eleven

Daniel Metwater paced the length of the conference room at Ranger Brigade headquarters, his dark, curly hair in disarray from continually raking his hands through it. He stopped and turned to face Jake and Carmen as they entered the room. "What took you so long?" he demanded.

"You could have returned to your camp, and we would have come to you there," Jake said. Metwater didn't look so in control of himself today. Dark circles beneath his eyes testified to a lack of sleep, and he stood with his shoulders hunched, as if anticipating a blow.

"It's not safe for me there." He jerked his head toward the door. "I've been trying to tell your colleagues, but they said I would have to wait for you."

Carmen pulled a chair out from the conference table. "Mr. Metwater, sit down, and we'll discuss this," she said.

He scowled at her. "If you'd been doing your job

instead of spying on me and my followers, you could have prevented this," he said.

"Prevented what?" Jake sat across from the chair Carmen had pulled out for Metwater. "Sit down, and start at the beginning. We can't help you if you're not making sense."

The scowl deepened, but Metwater dropped into the chair. "I need protection," he said.

"Protection from what?" Carmen filled a paper cup from the water cooler by the door and slid it across to Metwater, then sat beside Jake.

"The people who killed my brother. They're after me now." He drained the cup, then crumpled it in his fist. "Killing Reggae was a warning to me."

"Who are these people?" Jake asked.

"Organized crime. Russian organized crime. The *Bratva.*"

"The Chicago police suspected they were responsible for your brother's death, but they never found any proof," Carmen said.

"They killed him," Metwater said. "He was into them for too much. He was so reckless and stupid— he thought nothing could ever touch him. He embezzled almost a million dollars from our father, but it wasn't enough. He owed even more—gambling debts, women, drugs. If there was a vice, David had it."

"And you were the good brother," Jake said.

Metwater's eyes flashed with anger. "I wasn't a saint but, compared to David, I looked like one."

"Why do you think your brother's killers are after

you?" Carmen asked. "They took their revenge out on him, and they've left you alone until now."

He raked his hands through his hair again. "I don't know why now. I thought that, after all this time, they were satisfied, that David's blood was enough for them. Then they killed Reggae…"

"We haven't found anything to link organized crime to Reggae's murder," Jake said. "It's more likely that he died because he was involved with a man or men who are smuggling rare cactus off public land."

Metwater stiffened. "What men?" he asked.

"Do you know a man named Werner Altbusser, a German?" Jake asked.

"Do you think he killed Reggae?" Metwater asked.

"We don't know. Do you know him?"

Metwater's shoulders relaxed, though sweat beaded his forehead. "Not well. He came to my camp and asked my permission to recruit some of my followers to hunt for cactus for him. I told him I didn't care what they did. I don't control their lives."

"When did he ask you?" Jake asked.

"A few days ago. He approached me first about making a donation to my ministry."

"Did you accept the donation?" Carmen asked.

"The money was freely offered and freely accepted," he said. "There's no law against it."

"No, but I have to wonder if he was trying to influence your answer to his request," she said.

"My answer was immaterial."

"Was anyone else with Werner when you talked?" Jake asked.

"No. He was alone." He opened his fist and let the crumpled cup fall onto the table between them. "Werner isn't important. He didn't kill Reggae, the *Bratva* did. And I'm their next target. You have to protect me."

"I thought you had your own bodyguards," Carmen said.

He sent her another withering look. "The men who are after me are professional killers. I need professional protection."

"Then you should consider hiring private security," she said. "We can't devote officers to babysitting you on the basis of your own paranoia."

He shoved the chair back so hard it toppled as he stood, the sound of it striking the floor jarring. "You think I'm making this up—that I'm not in any danger."

"If you receive a threatening note or phone call, or have some other proof that your life is in danger, we'll work with you to keep you out of harm's way," Carmen said. "But we're not designed as a private security force."

"If you feel you're in real danger, perhaps you should relocate to someplace safer," Jake said.

"You'd like that, wouldn't you?" He leaned towards Jake, hands clenched at his sides. Jake braced himself for a blow, sure Metwater was going to hit him. But, at the last moment, the Prophet whirled away. "I should have known better than to come here for help," he shouted. "You'd be happy if I ended up dead!" He shoved past Jake and out the door.

Jake's ears rang in the silence that followed. He turned to Carmen. "What do you think?"

"I think he's really terrified," she said.

Marco and Ethan came in. "We heard part of the conversation," Marco said.

"You were listening at the door," Carmen said.

"It wasn't hard," Ethan said. "He was shouting half the time."

"Did anyone look into the mob angle?" Carmen asked.

"No one reported seeing anyone near the trailhead the morning Reggae was shot," Ethan said. "No suspicious cars."

"No swarthy men with foreign accents," Marco deadpanned.

"We had a botanist from Colorado Mesa University look at the cactus that were in the backpack," Ethan said. "Most of them were pretty common, but a few of them were rare enough to be of interest to a collector. So maybe Reggae knew what he was doing after all."

"Or maybe he just got lucky," Jake said. "Any sign of Werner?"

"All we can say is he hasn't visited the national park," Ethan said. "But that's the only place you need a permit to enter."

"He could be clear-cutting big swaths of the rest of the public land, and we'd never know about it if someone didn't complain," Marco added.

"It wouldn't hurt to run a few extra patrols around Metwater's camp," Carmen said. "See if you spot anything suspicious."

"And he can't say we're harassing him, since he practically begged us to protect him," Marco said.

"Carmen and I can check around there this afternoon," Jake said. "I need to talk to Starfall again, anyway. I want to know if she's made contact with Werner."

"Good luck getting her to admit to that," Carmen said.

He sent her a look that was supposed to communicate that he didn't care so much about Starfall—though he would talk to her. He needed to see Phoenix and Sophie and reassure himself that they were all right.

His cell phone buzzed, and he checked it but didn't recognize the number. Frowning, he answered the call. "Hello?"

"Jake, you have to come quick." A female voice sobbed out the words.

He gripped the phone tighter. "Sophie? Is that you?"

"Jake, you have to come. Mom fainted again, and it's really bad. I'm afraid she's dying!"

CARMEN GRIPPED THE armrest and tried to brace herself as the pickup truck jounced down the rutted road, yet with every bump she was thrown to the side or bounced in the air. "Wrecking your truck isn't going to get us there any faster," she said through gritted teeth.

Jake's grim expression didn't change, but he did let up on the gas a little. "I tried to get Sophie to call an ambulance," he said. "But she said Mom made her promise not to. If I have to, I'll put Mom in the truck and drive her to the hospital myself."

"How did Sophie manage to call you, anyway?" Carmen asked.

"She got Starfall to drive her to the café out by the lake, and she used their phone. She and Starfall are on their way back to camp now. I guess I owe Starfall for agreeing to take her. The poor kid was panicked."

"Maybe Starfall is trying to score points with you."

He glanced at her. "You're kidding, right? She hates me now that she knows I'm a cop."

"She knew you were a cop when she stole your badge, and that didn't stop her from pursuing you."

He shook his head, grinning.

"What are you smiling about?" she asked.

"You're jealous."

"I am not!" Just because the idea of Jake and Starfall together made her see red didn't mean she was jealous. She merely hated to see him taken in by such a manipulative woman. "I know Starfall doesn't do anything unless there's something in it for her."

"Maybe she likes my sister. Did you ever think of that?"

Carmen pressed her lips together. Sophie was certainly likable, but she didn't think Starfall had ever paid much attention to the girl. Better to let Jake think everyone loved his sister and wanted the best for her.

They arrived back at camp moments after Daniel Metwater. The Prophet turned to meet them, his expression guarded. "Have you decided to take my concerns seriously?" he asked.

"I'm not here for you," Jake said as he strode past Metwater. "I got a call from my sister that my mother fainted again."

Metwater hurried after Jake, with Carmen close behind. Asteria met them on the path. She grabbed Metwater's hand. "You're needed," she said and pulled him toward camp.

Jake put a hand on her arm to stop her. "Where's Phoenix?" he asked.

Asteria gave him a puzzled look. "She's in her trailer, I guess."

"What do you mean, you guess?" He looked as if he wanted to shake her. Carmen laid a pacifying hand on his arm, and he released the other woman. "Sophie called me in a panic. She said Phoenix fainted again."

"She did. But she's fine now."

"What did you need me for?" Metwater asked.

"There's someone here to see you. He's waiting in your trailer."

Metwater froze. "Who is he?"

Asteria glanced at Carmen and Jake, then back to Metwater. "He's a…a business associate. He was here once before."

Metwater turned to Jake and Carmen. "You have to come with me," he said.

"I have to see my mother," Jake said.

Metwater grabbed his arm. "You have to protect me."

"Protect you from what?" Jake shook him off. "Who is your visitor?"

"I think it's that German—Altbusser." He glanced at Asteria, and she nodded.

"You said yourself he isn't the killer," Jake said.

"Maybe I was wrong. Maybe he's an assassin, sent to kill me." Metwater's voice shook, and his eyes were wide with panic.

"Then don't talk to him," Jake said. "I have to see my mother."

Carmen hesitated, debating staying with Metwater or going with Jake. Jake looked back at her. "I need your help," he said. The worry and fear in his eyes won her over. Metwater's danger might be all in his head, but Jake had real reason to be concerned for his mother.

Sarah met them at the door of Phoenix's trailer. "She's better now," Sarah said. "At first we were so worried because, after she came to from this last fainting spell, she wasn't herself. She was running a fever and out of her head, talking nonsense. That's when Sophie insisted on calling you."

Jake moved through the trailer's small living and kitchen areas to the bedroom. Phoenix lay on her back in the middle of the bed, her arms folded across her chest and her eyes closed. Carmen bit back a cry—for a moment the older woman looked as if she was laid out for a funeral.

"Mom, it's me, Jake," he said softly. Carmen glanced at him and felt a tightness in her chest. In that moment, the scared boy showed beneath the surface of the tough, courageous man.

Phoenix opened her eyes. "What are you doing here, son?" she asked.

"Sophie called and told me you were sick."

"She shouldn't have done that." She tried to prop herself up on her elbows but fell back with a sigh.

Jake sat on the edge of the bed and took her hand. "Mom, you need to see a doctor," he said. "Fainting like this and being this weak isn't right. Sarah said you were delirious when you came to."

"I'm just tired, that's all," Phoenix said. "And I wasn't delirious. Sarah exaggerates." She looked past him to Carmen. "Hello, dear."

"Hello, Phoenix." Carmen drew closer. "I talked to my aunt this morning," she said. "She's a nurse at the Ute tribal clinic. She thinks you could just be anemic. It's easy to fix, but you need to see the doctor to make sure you get the right treatment."

Phoenix's lower lip trembled. "But what if it's not just anemia? What if it's something worse?"

"Then you'll get the right treatment for that."

Carmen took Phoenix's other hand. "You're a very strong woman. Think of all you've overcome already. You're not going to let something like a little illness stop you."

"I don't feel so strong lately," Phoenix said.

"Please, Mom," Jake said. "If you won't go for yourself, do it for me and Sophie."

"You need to go to the doctor, Mama."

Carmen and Jake turned and saw Sophie standing in the doorway of the bedroom. Her face was pale, and she had obviously been crying. But now she looked angry. She glared at her mother. "You scared me. I thought you were dying, and there was nothing I could do. I don't want to lose you."

She choked back a sob. Jake stood and started toward her, but Phoenix managed to shove herself into a sitting position. She held out her arms. "Come here, baby," she said.

Sophie ran to her mother and buried her face against her shoulder. Phoenix stroked her hair. "It's okay, sweetie," she murmured. "You don't have to get so upset. I'll go see someone at the clinic in town." She looked up at Jake. "You can make the appointment for me. And I want you and Carmen both to go with me."

The request startled Carmen. After all, she wasn't family, or even particularly close to Phoenix. "Are you sure you want me along?" she asked.

"Absolutely." A hint of a smile curved her lips. "Someone has to keep Jake from getting upset about something and flying off the handle. You seem to have a calming effect on him."

Her eyes met Jake's, and she could tell he was thinking the same thing she was—that *calming* wasn't the word she would use to describe the effect they had on each other. *Ravenous* or *incendiary* might be better terms, considering the way they had gone after each other on the bluff on her family's ranch. Her face felt hot just remembering their lovemaking. She usually wasn't so reckless, but after a morning spent facing other people's expectations of her—her mother's and Rodney's and even Aunt Connie's—she had wanted to revel in the freedom of being with someone who had no expectations.

Jake accepted her as she was. To him, she wasn't the beauty queen or the tough cop or the obedient daughter or niece. She was merely herself. Someone he freely admitted he wanted to be with, someone with no ulterior motive or guile. He might be skilled at deceiving people, but she was pretty sure he wasn't being deceptive when he said he liked her and was attracted to her.

Somewhere between that first kiss and her crying out her climax, Jake Lohmiller had touched more than her skin. He had touched her heart.

Chapter Twelve

Jake told himself he ought to feel good about getting his mother to agree to see the doctor, but he couldn't shake off the pain of seeing her so frail and helpless. He didn't want to have to deal with that, so he tried to push the memory away. Time to focus on work—something he was better at controlling.

"We should stop by Metwater's motor home and see what Werner wants."

"I want to talk to Starfall first," he said. "It won't hurt Metwater to see that we're not at his beck and call. And we can see Metwater's motorhome from her tent. Werner won't leave without us knowing about it."

"What if Metwater is in real danger?"

"If I thought that was true, I would have been over there before now," he said. "But he hasn't given us one scrap of evidence to prove there's a real threat." He glanced around them. "Tony is supposed to be watching Werner, so he's probably around here somewhere. He'll act if there's trouble. And Metwater always has a couple of young guys hanging around as muscle, and we know he owns at least one gun. I think he can look after himself for a few more minutes. So he can wait."

He headed toward the white tent Starfall shared with Asteria. Carmen followed. He couldn't tell if her silence meant she agreed with him or if she was only putting up with him because this was technically his investigation. She wasn't a person who wore her emotions on her sleeve, which he liked most of the time, but it did make it tougher for him to read her.

Starfall stepped outside, her baby in her arms, as the two officers approached. She said nothing, only glowered as they drew near.

"Thank you for helping my sister and my mom," Jake said. "I really appreciate it."

Her expression softened. She shifted the baby to one hip and some of the stiffness went out of her posture. "Is Phoenix going to be okay?" she asked.

"I hope so," he said. "She agreed to let me make an appointment at the clinic in town."

"What about Sophie?" Starfall bounced the baby. "She was pretty upset."

"She'll be okay, too."

"She's a tough kid. Like her mom." She sent him a sideways glance. "And her brother, I guess."

"Have you talked to Werner lately?" he asked.

The guarded expression returned. "I don't know anyone named Werner."

"Yes, you do. The German who asked you to collect cactus for him?"

"I don't see that it's any of your business who I talk to." The Starfall he knew best was back, all tough attitude and pout.

Jake ground his teeth in frustration. He couldn't tell her Werner was on his radar as a lawbreaker; he might have said too much already. And his original plan to pay Starfall for information about the German wasn't going to work, either. She didn't strike him as the type to resist the temptation to double-cross. She would take his money, then turn around and sell any information he passed on to Werner for more money. Better to let her go on working for the German and keep an eye on her to see what she led him to. "I was wondering if he needed any more cactus," he said. "I saw some good specimens near where I was camped before. If you're still selling them to him, you might look there."

Her eyes lit up. "Thanks. I may walk over there tomorrow and check them out." She shifted the baby again. "Maybe you're not so bad—for a cop."

"Yeah," he said. "For a cop."

He turned to walk away. "Hey, Soldier Boy," she called after him.

He looked over his shoulder at her. "What?"

"I hope your mom gets better soon."

The tightness in his chest returned—the pain that he had felt when he'd seen his mother lying in her bed, looking so small and frail and helpless. For all the mistakes she had made and the bad things she had done, his mom had always been so full of life and energy. He did love her. At times, he had thought he hated her. But he had never been afraid for her, the way he was now. "Thanks," he said. "I hope so, too."

He headed toward Metwater's trailer, Carmen beside him. She didn't have to say anything—just having her there with him made him feel calmer. "Thanks for telling Mom about what your aunt said," he told her. "I think it helped."

"Maybe." She glanced at him. "This can't be easy for you."

"Life with Mom has never been easy." He shrugged off the memories. "But that's in the past. I just want to make the future better—for her, but especially for Sophie."

"You've already helped your mother and sister, by coming back into their lives," Carmen said.

"I hope that's true." He couldn't be sure. "I was away for too long," he said.

"My grandfather always said guilt was a prison you built yourself."

"Is that some bit of tribal wisdom?" Jake asked.

"I don't think so. I think he read it in a magazine or something."

He laughed, surprised that he felt so much better. "Mom was right about you," he said.

She looked wary. "What about me?"

"You know just how to handle me."

A pink flush warmed her skin, and he wondered

if she was thinking of the way she had handled him earlier.

She was the first to look away. "Let's go talk to Metwater and his visitor," she said.

Asteria admitted them without comment. Metwater sat in his recliner, stiffly upright, while Werner sat on the sofa beside him. Jake was thankful he was in civilian clothes today. He only hoped Metwater wouldn't blow his cover by revealing he was a cop.

Werner started to stand, then sank back onto the sofa. For once, Metwater looked relieved to see the officers. "These are a couple of friends," he said by way of introduction. "Mr. Altbusser is an associate of mine who is in the area on vacation and stopped by to say hello."

Jake nodded to Werner. "Mr. Altbusser and I ran into each other when I was camping not far from here," he said. "How is your vacation going?"

"I may have to cut my visit short," Werner said. "But I appreciate the Prophet giving me another audience before I had to leave. I am very interested in his experiment in cooperative living here in the desert."

Jake supposed that was one way to describe what Metwater was doing out here in the wilderness. "Why do you have to shorten your visit?" he asked.

"A business crisis I must see to." Werner waved away the question. "I have already asked Mr. Metwater, but I will ask you, too. I was hoping to meet up with a friend of mine who I understand is also visiting in the area, but so far I haven't been able to find him. Perhaps you have seen him."

"Who is your friend?" Jake asked.

"He is a Russian. Taller than me, and broader. His name is Karol Petrovsky. We worked together once upon a time. I only just heard he was in the area."

At the mention of the Russian, Metwater paled. Jake ignored him and shook his head. "Sorry, I haven't seen him. He sounds like the kind of guy I would remember."

"Yes, he is very memorable." Werner shrugged. "If I do not find him, then perhaps it was not meant to be." He stood and offered his hand to Metwater. "I will not take up any more of your time," he said.

Metwater let the German take his hand, then Werner insisted on shaking hands with Jake and Carmen as well, before one of the bodyguards escorted him from the motor home.

As soon as Werner was gone, Metwater leaned toward Jake and spoke in an urgent whisper. "Did you hear him? This Russian must be the killer who's after me."

"Not every Russian is a member of the Russian mafia," Jake said.

Metwater glared at him. "You can't think this is merely a coincidence."

"Life is full of coincidences," Jake said. "But we will keep an eye out for this Russian. If the man was a friend of Werner's, he might be involved in the same smuggling operation."

"Was that all Mr. Altbusser wanted?" Carmen asked. "To ask about his friend?"

"What else would he want?" Metwater asked.

"Maybe he wanted to recruit more of your followers to find cactus for him," she said. "Maybe he even offered you a cut of the profits."

"I have better things to do with my time than dig up plants." He stood. "If you're not going to help me, you can leave."

That was fine with Jake. "Call us if Werner visits again," he said. "Or if you spot any Russians—mafia or otherwise."

He and Carmen left. He was silent until they were back in his truck. "Starfall won't be happy if she finds out she has to compete with other people for payment from Werner," he said.

"I'm guessing if Werner did make an offer, Metwater won't go for it now," Carmen said. "He's too afraid of Werner's friend, the Russian."

"There's something else about this whole setup that bothers me," Jake said.

"Only one thing?"

"One other thing," he said. "Where is Tony?"

"Tony?" she asked.

"He's the Fish and Wildlife agent who took my place. The man who's supposed to be shadowing Werner? I didn't spot him anywhere around camp."

"He's not supposed to let Werner see him," she said. "Maybe he was doing a really good job."

"I would have spotted him," Jake said. He pressed down on the accelerator, speeding up.

Carmen grabbed hold of the dash as they bounced over the rough road. "What are you doing?" she asked.

"We have to go to Werner's motel," he said. "Tony had a room there. We have to make sure he's all right."

SOPHIE KICKED AT the dirt outside the trailer. As soon as Jake and Carmen left, Sarah had sent her away. "Go play now," she said, shooing her toward the door. "Your mother needs to rest." As if Sophie was some little kid and couldn't help take care of her own mother.

Her mom looked bad. At least she wasn't out of her head, the way she had been when she first woke up after her fainting spell. At least Jake had been able to talk her into seeing a doctor. She sure hoped there was some medicine that could make her better. Sophie had never minded much not having her father around, but what would she do without her mother?

And, of course, doctors didn't work for free. They'd need money to pay for the treatments and medicine her mother might need. Maybe the Prophet would pay for them. He always talked about how they were a *Family*, and families shared everything and took care of each other. But sharing a pot of beans was a lot different from sharing medical bills. Her mother had signed over everything to him when they had joined the Family, but it wasn't like it had been a lot—an old car that wasn't even around anymore and the trailer they lived in. Her mother had never held a steady job, and they had never had any money. That hadn't mattered so much most of the time. She and Sophie had lived with Grandma and Grandpa, and then here with the Prophet. But medical bills were different. They could be hundreds, thousands of dollars, maybe even more. The Prophet might not want to pay that much.

She wandered away from the trailer, toward the center of camp. Times like this she missed having someone her own age around. When Jake talked of her going to school and having friends, it sounded fun. Back when she had lived with her grandparents, she had liked school, and she had been starting to make friends when her mother decided they should move. She imagined it would be like in books she had read—she would have two or three best friends, or even just one—and they would have sleepovers and stuff like that. It made a little ache around her heart when she thought about it, so most of the time she tried to put the idea out of her mind.

"Hey, Sophie! Come here a minute!"

She looked around and saw Starfall beckoning her from outside her tent. Sophie started toward her. She didn't really like Starfall all that much—she was too bossy and even mean sometimes. But her little boy, Hunter, was so sweet, and he liked Sophie a lot. He always smiled and held out his arms to her when she was near. Maybe Starfall wanted Sophie to watch him while she went off with her friends or some guy. Sophie usually didn't mind babysitting—it was something to do, after all. But this time, maybe she'd ask if Starfall could pay her. She needed to start earning money in case her mom needed it.

But Hunter wasn't with Starfall, who sat in a folding chair outside her tent, one foot propped up on the edge of the chair while she painted the toenails a bright pink. "What are you up to?" Starfall asked when Sophie stopped in front of her.

Sophie shrugged. "Not much. Do you need me to watch Hunter?"

"Not now. He's napping." She capped the bottle of polish and fanned her hand over her toenails. "Do you remember that cactus you found for me the other day? The day we were picking berries?"

"You mean the day the guy shot at us?"

Starfall frowned. "Well, yeah, that too."

Sophie wanted to laugh. How could anybody think cactus were more memorable than being shot at? But that was Starfall—she was going to make money off cactus, so that was what was most important to her. "Yeah, I remember," she said.

"Your brother said he saw more of them by where he was camped. Do you think you could find them for me?"

Interesting that Jake had been talking to Starfall. But maybe it was the other way around. Starfall liked to flirt with men. Maybe she had been flirting with

Jake. But Jake was interested in Carmen—anybody could see that. Just another example of Starfall being clueless. "I don't know where he was camped," Sophie said.

"I do." Starfall lowered her foot to the ground and extended both legs to admire her freshly painted toes. "We can walk over there in the morning, and I'll show you."

"What will you give me if I find the cactus for you?" Sophie asked.

"Why should I give you anything?" Starfall asked.

"Didn't you say some guy is paying you for the cactus? If I'm doing the work, I should get part of the money."

Starfall narrowed her eyes, but she must have seen that Sophie wasn't going to back down. "I'll give you five dollars," she said.

"I want ten."

"No way," Starfall said. "That's half of what I make. And I'm a lot older than you are."

"But I'm the one who'll be doing all the work—finding and digging," Sophie said. "Besides, with me along, you'll find more cactus. Maybe twice as much."

Starfall had to know this was true. By herself, she wasn't patient enough to crawl around in the hot sun and really look at the plants on the ground. She would much rather have Sophie do everything for her. The older woman looked sullen but nodded.

"Okay. But you don't get the money until after Werner pays me."

Sophie would rather have had the money up front. She didn't trust Starfall not to "forget" to pay her. But if that happened, she would ask Jake to get the money for her. She doubted very many people would say no to her brother when he was angry. Mama always scolded Jake for having a bad temper, but maybe sometimes it was a good thing. "All right," she said.

"Good. Meet me back here after breakfast," Starfall said. "Bring something to dig with and a sack to put everything in."

Sophie could have argued that if she was going to do all the work, she shouldn't have to provide the tools, too, but since she was getting ten dollars, she kept quiet. "All right. I'll see you in the morning." She turned away, not letting Starfall see how happy she was. She would find as many cactus as she could tomorrow. Ten—maybe even twenty. That would be a couple hundred dollars to help pay her mom's doctor bills. Jake would be so impressed. He wouldn't treat her like a baby who couldn't be counted on to help out when it really mattered.

JAKE BROKE EVERY speed limit on the way to the motel where Werner and Tony were staying—the motel where Jake had also stayed in order to shadow Werner until Tony had taken over that job. He circled around to the back of the motel and cruised past the room where Werner was staying—151. Tony would be in Jake's old room, 153, right next door. "That's Werner's rental," he said, indicating the red Jeep parked in front of 151.

"Do you see Tony's car?" Carmen asked.

"I don't know what he's driving. But he wouldn't have it parked in front of his room, anyway. He wouldn't want Werner to see it and recognize it, if he had to follow the suspect later." He parked his truck facing a fence across from the two rooms and shut off the engine, then sat, his hands on the steering wheel, eyes fixed on the image of the two motel-room doors in his rearview mirror.

"What now?" Carmen asked.

"I can't risk Werner seeing me and wondering what I'm doing here," he said. "Maybe you should go knock on Tony's door, see if he's in."

"Werner has seen me."

"But not for long." He reached behind the seat and pulled out a Houston Astros ball cap. "Stuff your hair under this, and keep your sunglasses on. Slouch or shuffle or something to change your gait. Approach the room from the side, so Werner can't get a good look at you out the window."

She took the cap. "What do I do if Tony answers? How will I even recognize him?"

"He's shorter than me and stockier. Balding. Crooked nose where it was broken a long time ago. Tell him you're with me, and ask him to meet us somewhere near here in half an hour."

"All right." She gathered her long, black hair at the nape of her neck and twisted it into a coil, then covered the coil with the cap. This exposed her neck, and he fought the urge to lean over and kiss that long, smooth column. She put her hand on the door to open it, and he reached out and squeezed her arm.

"Be careful," he said. "If you see anything out of line, get out of there ASAP."

"I know the drill," she said. "I've been a cop a while now."

"Right." He let go of her. He forgot sometimes that she had more experience than he did.

He kept her in view as she moved behind the line of parked cars, then crossed the parking lot and walked toward Tony's room, approaching it from the direction opposite Werner's door. She pulled the hat lower over her eyes, then knocked on the door of 153. She waited a long minute. Jake gripped the steering wheel, counting off the seconds. If Werner was in his room—and the presence of his Jeep indicated he was—why wasn't Tony answering his door?

Carmen lifted her hand to knock again, and at that moment the door to the room swung inward. A man ran out, knocking Carmen back onto the sidewalk. She struggled with him as Jake bailed out of the truck, reaching for the gun tucked into the back of his jeans.

The man, a bulky build whose face was turned away from Jake, hauled back and punched Carmen in the face. Jake felt the punch in his own gut and raised his gun. "Stop! Police!" he shouted.

Carmen's assailant didn't even look his way. He jumped up and ducked behind the nearest car, then took off running. Jake pursued, his feet pounding the asphalt lot, but the man was too far ahead of him. He didn't see his quarry get into a vehicle, but the roar of an engine and the squeal of tires announced his getaway as he sped out of the motel lot and into traffic on the highway.

Jake stared after the fleeing vehicle—a dark SUV with heavily tinted windows. Mud on the license plate made it impossible to read. By the time he reached his truck to chase him, the man would be long gone. He turned and jogged back toward Carmen, picking up speed when he saw her still lying on the concrete. His heart battered his ribs as he threw himself down beside her. "Carmen, are you okay?"

She opened her eyes and looked up at him. "Did you get the linebacker who ran over me?" she asked.

He laughed—a sick sound full of relief and agony. "He got away," he said. "Are you okay? Should I call an ambulance?"

"He just knocked the wind out of me." She tugged on his hand and pulled herself into a sitting position. She touched the corner of her eye, which was already swelling and darkening where the assailant had hit her, and she winced. "I think it was Werner's friend—the Russian. The description fit, anyway."

Jake looked back at 153. The door stood open, the

interior of the room in deep shadow. "I don't have a good feeling about this," he said.

"He was in a hurry to get out of there." Carmen tried to stand and swayed a little.

Jake jumped up and held onto her. "You should sit down."

"I'll be fine." She swatted him away. "We'd better call for backup."

"You call." He made sure she was braced against the side of the building and released her. "I'm going to check inside." He wasn't going to stand around waiting when Tony might be still alive and hurt, needing help right away.

She pulled out her phone. "All right. But be careful."

The same words he had used with her. Words cops said to each other all the time, overstating the obvious. They were always careful—but not too careful. Part of the job was taking risks most sensible people wouldn't take.

Avoiding touching anyplace that might retain prints, he nudged open the door with the toe of his boot. Sunlight arced into the small room, revealing an overturned chair and an unmade bed, the flower-print bedspread half-trailing onto the gray-green carpeting. He pulled out his phone and used the flashlight app to illuminate the rest of the room. He stilled on a bright red smear on the far wall and followed it down to the floor—and the body of Field Agent Tony Davidson.

Chapter Thirteen

Carmen ignored the aches and pains in her face and limbs as she stood beside Jake and watched paramedics carry Tony's body out of the motel room on a draped stretcher. His throat had been cut—a brutal, terrifying way to die. "I'm sorry about your friend," she said to Jake as the doors of the ambulance closed.

"He wasn't a friend. Not really."

"But another agent—they're a little like family."

"Yeah." He brushed his finger over the bruise on her cheek, and a shiver ran through her. "I saw red when that guy knocked you down."

"I'm okay. I've been hurt worse. I'm guessing he was the killer, but why?"

"I don't know. Tony was a good agent. I don't see how the Russian—if that was the Russian—could have made him for a cop. But I knew if he wasn't on the job, something must have happened to him."

"Did you think Werner did something to him before he headed out to see Metwater?"

Jake shook his head. "I didn't know. I just had a

bad feeling. I was hoping we'd get here and find him sick with the flu or something."

She glanced toward the room next door. Jake had pointed it out to her earlier as Werner's room. "Do we know Werner is in there?" she asked.

"We're pretty sure. That's his vehicle in front of the door."

"You'd think he would come out to see what all the commotion is about."

"He probably looked out and saw the police cars and is lying low. But I'd sure like to know how much he knows about all this."

"Then why don't you question him?" she asked.

"Because then he would know I'm a cop. When I called in to tell my boss what was going on, he told me to get away from here as soon as I could, and to not let Werner see me. He's hoping if I stay undercover—at least until they get an agent here to replace Tony—we can avoid aborting the investigation. We've been working on this case for more than a year and have poured thousands of dollars into it. We're really close to making a bunch of arrests."

"I can ask one of the other Rangers to question him." Carmen said. "He can say he's interviewing everyone near the victim's room."

"Good idea," Jake said.

"Let's call Lance Carpenter." She pulled out her phone. "Being with the Montrose Sheriff's Department, he won't look out of place."

Since the Sheriff's Department already had their

investigative team on site, this made sense. Fish and Wildlife would assign someone to the case as well—maybe even Jake. But for now, they were relying on the local cops to secure the evidence on scene.

Carmen gave Lance a summary of what was going on, then passed the phone to Jake, who provided more background on Werner and what they hoped to learn from him. He gave Lance his contact information, then hung up and returned the phone to Carmen. "He's on his way. Let me take you back to your place. You need to put some ice on that eye."

CARMEN'S PLACE TURNED out to be half of a duplex not far from the national park. "We call this Ranger Row, so many of us live here," she said as Jake pulled his truck into her driveway. "Or used to. Marco and Michael and Randall have all gotten married recently and moved into town with their wives. But there are still some of us diehards around."

He followed her up the walk from the driveway and waited while she unlocked the door. A loud yowl greeted them as they stepped inside. "I know, Muffin. I've been away forever." She stooped and gathered up a yellow tabby, who rubbed his head against her chin, then eyed Jake over her shoulder.

"You have a cat," he said, hanging back a little.

"I've had Muffin since he was a kitten." She cradled the cat in her arms and rubbed under his chin. The cat arched his neck and let out a purr that was audible across the room. She glanced at him. "You don't have a problem with cats, do you?"

"I've never been around them much." Not at all, really.

"Well, come and say hello."

Jake approached cautiously. Muffin watched him through slit, golden eyes. He held out his hand, letting the animal sniff him. That was what you were supposed to do, right? Then he let out a yelp as Muffin sank his teeth into Jake's thumb.

"Muffin, no!" Carmen scolded. She set the cat on the floor and turned to Jake. "Are you okay? I don't know what got into him."

Jake sucked him thumb and eyed the cat, who was stalking away, looking back every few paces to glare at Jake. So that was how it was going to be, was it? "I think maybe he's a little, um, possessive."

Carmen wrinkled her forehead. "Why would you think that?"

Because I'm the guy who wants to keep him from being the only male in your life. "I have no idea," he said. He walked over to a bookcase, where she had a number of pictures displayed in frames. Several showed her with various family members—her mother, a man he assumed was her father, her aunt and others. In one, she stood in the center of a group of women, all dressed in Native American dresses decorated with feathers and bells. "What is this?" he asked.

"I used to dance at powwows, when I was a teen-ager."

He grinned. "I'd like to see that some time."

He started to reach for her, but she turned away. "Do you want something to drink? I've got tea and sodas in the kitchen." She was already moving toward the kitchen, and he hurried to catch up with her.

Like the rest of the house, the kitchen was small but neat, decorated in red and yellow. She was opening a can of cat food when he entered the room. "I'd better feed Muffin before he starts complaining," she said.

At the sound of his name, the cat came into the room, again glaring at Jake as he passed him. Jake liked that the cat saw him as a threat. Animals were supposed to be sensitive to emotions, right? So maybe he was picking up on Carmen's feelings for this intruder. Or maybe that was Jake's wishful thinking.

Cat fed, she moved to putting ice in glasses. "Would you rather have a beer or something?"

He put his hand on hers to stop her. "I don't need anything," he said.

She looked up, her eyes big and dark. Her hand trembled a little. "You're nervous," he said, the idea shocking him. He moved his hand away and stepped back. "Why?"

She ducked her head, her hair falling forward in a silken curtain that hid her expression from him.

"I guess I'm feeling a little…vulnerable, having you here."

"Do you want me to go?" His stomach knotted, but he forced himself to keep his voice even.

"No!" She turned away from the counter and reached for him.

He slipped two fingers beneath her chin and tilted her face up until he could look into her eyes. It bothered him a little to see the one eye swollen shut. "We forgot the ice for your eye," he said.

"A little late for that now. It's okay."

"Then want to tell me what the problem is? Why do you feel vulnerable?"

She blew out a breath. "I'm a cop. And I work with men all day. The criminals I deal with are mostly men. To deal with that—to fit in and do my job— I've learned to be tough. A little hard. And it's a side effect of the job that I tend to deal with all people that way. Makes it hard to date but, I figure, if a guy wants to be with me, he's got to accept that."

"You don't seem hard to me." He traced his finger along the underside of her jaw, and the soft, satiny skin there. She closed her eyes and leaned into his hand—not unlike her cat had done with her earlier.

"That's just it—you've made me let my guard down. Something I didn't see coming. I'm not sure I know how to handle it."

"You're doing a good job so far." He kissed her cheek, and then her smooth, warm throat, slipping one hand around her back to draw her snug against him.

She looked into his eyes, searching. "Part of me says not to trust you."

That hurt to hear, but he wasn't going to run from it. "Why is that?"

"Because you're not like any other man I've known. You don't have ties to a group of people or a certain place. You have your mother and sister and your job, but you still seem so alone."

"I am alone, but I'm trying to change that. I came to get my mother and sister to change that. I think I'm attracted to you because I want to change that."

"Can you change?" she asked. "Can a loner become part of a group? Part of a family?"

"If it's the right group. The right family." He kissed her temple, and she closed her eyes, then stood on tiptoe and pressed her lips to his.

"Then I want to help you try," she whispered. She took his hand in hers and tugged him away from the counter.

She led him out of the room and down a short hallway to her bedroom. He had an impression of soft blues and muted light before she closed the door behind them and gathered him in her arms.

"Just so you know, your being tough never put me off," he said. "It's one of the things that attracted me to you from that first day."

"I figured most men like to play Big Strong Rescuer." She smoothed her hand down his back. "More than one man has told me I'm too intimidating."

"It can be an ego stroke to save someone but,

you know, I did enough rescuing of my mom. I like a woman who can stand on her own feet—or who could rescue me, if that's what I needed." He kissed the corner of her mouth. "Or, as my mom pointed out, one who can keep me in line."

He liked the way her eyes crinkled when she smiled. She grasped the pull of his zipper. "I like keeping you in line," she said as she slowly lowered it.

He caught his breath as she freed him from his jeans and underwear, then he began undoing the buttons of her shirt. "Can't let you have all the fun," he murmured.

Their first lovemaking had been hurried, almost frantic in the rush to satisfy their pent-up need. This time, they savored the experience, undressing slowly, becoming acquainted with the curves and planes of each other's bodies. He measured the weight of her breasts in his hands and the curve of her hip against his palm, savored the taste of her skin and the sound of the breathy moans she made as he kissed his way down her body.

In turn, she skimmed her hands along his shoulders and down his back, her touch sending shock waves of sensation through him. He focused all his attention on her, on her pleasure. Some of the urgency of that first time returned. Her climax was still shuddering through her when he levered himself over and into her. She wrapped her long legs around him and rocked with him in a rhythm that soon had him panting and on the edge of losing control.

She opened her eyes and met his gaze. "Let go," she whispered, and he did, waves of pleasure rocketing through him until he was utterly spent.

Afterwards, they lay together, his head resting on her shoulder, her fingers idly combing through his hair. He had never felt this close to anyone before— maybe he hadn't allowed himself to be this close. "Thank you," he said.

She rolled toward him and looked into his eyes. "What are you thanking me for?"

"For trusting me enough to let me into your life. I know it isn't easy. It isn't easy for me, either."

She rolled back. "You're tough to resist," she said. "And I usually have a lot of willpower."

He was trying to think of the right response to this when his phone rang. "Is that yours?" she asked.

"Yeah." Reluctantly, he got up and found his pants on the floor and retrieved the phone. "Hello?"

"It's Lance. I thought you'd want to know the results of my interview with Werner Altbusser."

The fog cleared and he tensed. "Tell me."

"About what you would expect—he doesn't know anything, he didn't see anything. But it's clear he's terrified of something. He was packing to leave when I got there. I told him that we needed him to stick around for a few days as a potential witness. I didn't come out and say we wouldn't let him leave, but I gave the strong impression, so I think he'll stay put.

Just in case he decides to bolt, I alerted all the airports in the area, and the Amtrak station in Grand Junction. If he tries to leave that way, they'll hold him for us."

"Thanks," Jake said "Did anybody else see the guy who did this?"

"No. Most of the rooms on that side of the motel are empty, or the occupants were out. No security cameras focused on that area, either. We've got an APB out with the description you gave us, but so far no one has spotted him."

"Werner mentioned this guy was camping in the wilderness area," Jake said. "If he wants to hide, it would be easier to do it there."

"We'll do some extra patrols and alert the park rangers and Forest Service people, too."

"Thanks."

"No problem. We want this guy as much as you do."

Jake ended the call with Lance and hit the number for his boss. Ron Clark answered on the second ring. "What have you got for us?" he asked.

He gave him a summary of Lance's report. "I was hoping you would have something," he said.

"We have a tentative ID on the Russian." Jake heard the tap of computer keys. "Karol Petrovsky. Originally from Vladivostok, but he's lived in Tokyo for the past ten years. We suspect he was Werner's Asian distributor. As far as we can determine, Petro-

vsky has never traveled to the United States before—
he left that side of the business to Altbusser."

"So what is he doing in the States now?" Jake
asked.

"We don't know. Maybe he wanted a bigger cut of
the profits. Or maybe he suspects Werner has been
cheating him."

"Werner seems afraid of the guy," Jake said. "Like
maybe they aren't friends anymore."

"Maybe he wants to eliminate Werner and get all
the business for himself," Clark said. "It's a profit-
able market, but a relatively small one—not room
for a lot of players."

"He must have killed Tony because he made him
as a cop," Jake said. "And he probably killed Reggae as a warning to Werner, or maybe he thought he
was eliminating more competition."

"Apparently, he did time in a Russian prison for
knifing a guy he thought had crossed him in a different business deal," Clark said.

Jake's stomach churned. "We've got to stop him."

"Watch your back," Clark said. "Clearly, he's ruth-
less. Keep tabs on him, but don't be a hero."

"Right." That was the sensible way to approach
this. But anyone who knew Jake would vouch for
the fact that he wasn't always sensible, especially
when it came to righting a wrong or protecting those
he loved.

Chapter Fourteen

The next morning, Sophie set out with Starfall to look for cactus. Starfall led the way toward the canyon where they had picked raspberries. "I thought we were going over by Jake's camp," Sophie said as they trudged along.

"That was too far to go this morning. We'll go tomorrow."

"I'm hoping tomorrow Jake will take Mom to the doctor." Phoenix was out of bed and said she felt better today, but Sophie didn't think she looked much better.

"We'll go the next day, then. Now hurry up." Starfall marched along the edge of the canyon, whacking berry vines out of her way with a machete she must have taken from the communal tool shed.

"But we already looked here," Sophie said. "That day we picked berries."

"We didn't look very long," Starfall said. "We were interrupted, remember?"

"Yeah." Sophie wasn't going to forget that. "Why do you think someone was shooting at us?"

"Your brother's the cop. Doesn't he know?"

"If he does, he didn't say." She bit her lower lip. "I wonder if it's the same guy who killed Reggae." She shivered, the thought both horrifying—and a little exciting.

"Well, he's not going to care about us." Starfall nudged her. "Don't worry about that. Look for cactus."

Sophie focused her eyes on the ground, searching for the little spiny plants. The sheet of paper Starfall had shown her earlier indicated they could be as small as a quarter, and almost the color of the soil. No wonder they were hard to find. "What are you going to do with the money you get for selling the cactus?" she asked.

Starfall shrugged. "I don't know."

"I thought maybe you were saving up to leave the camp."

Starfall crouched to examine the ground more closely. "Why do you think that?"

"I don't know." She turned over a fallen branch with her foot and studied the beetle that crawled from beneath it. "You're not like some of the others, making such a big deal over the Prophet. You seem more, I don't know, independent."

"I'll take that as a compliment," Starfall said. She rose and walked on. "Sometimes I think about traveling, or maybe starting my own business. But for now, I have it pretty good. I always liked camping, and the Prophet leaves me alone. He knows I'm not one of his groupies."

Sophie guessed that meant her mom was one of the Prophet's "groupies." It made Sophie feel a little icky to think about it. "Mom says he wants to marry me when I'm older." It was one of the things her mom had said when she was delirious after the last time she fainted, so Sophie didn't know if it was true—she hoped not.

Starfall gave her a hard look. "No offense, but your mom is dreaming," she said. "Daniel Metwater has no reason to marry one woman when he can have all the women he wants."

"I think it's creepy that a man as old as he is would even be interested in a fourteen-year-old," Sophie said, relieved to be able to say the words out loud. "But Mom doesn't see it that way."

"Your mom is a dreamer," Starfall said again. "Some people are like that. Maybe real life is too hard for them, so they make up a better one in their head. And I don't know—maybe she has the right idea. Everybody copes in her own way."

"Yeah, I guess so."

Starfall nudged her. "Your brother, now, he's the practical sort," she said. "He's not going to let the Prophet marry you, no matter what your mother says."

"Yeah. Jake is pretty great. I like Carmen, too."

"I don't trust Carmen, but then I don't trust most people."

"You don't trust her because she's a cop," Sophie said. And maybe because Carmen and Jake were a couple—or, at least, Sophie was pretty sure they were—and Starfall was jealous. Even a fourteen-year-old could see that.

"Whatever." Starfall looked at her. "What about you? What are you going to do with your share of the cactus money?"

"I need the money to help pay for Mom's doctor bills." She knelt and pointed to the ground. "And there's our first one."

Starfall took a trowel from the bag she had slung over her shoulder and handed it to Sophie. "One down, more to go."

In the next hour, they found only one more of the kind of cactus the German wanted. "I don't see what difference it makes what kind we get," Starfall said when they sat to rest in the shade of a rock. "They all look pretty much the same to me—ugly."

"I guess it makes a difference to whoever he's selling them to." Sophie tugged on the end of her braid and squinted across the empty landscape of rocks and juniper. "It's kind of creepy out here, don't you think?"

"What do you mean?"

"I don't know. It feels like someone's watching us." She shivered and rubbed her shoulders.

Starfall looked around them. "I don't see any-one," she said.

"If someone is spying on us, he wouldn't want us to see him, would he? It just doesn't feel right out here today."

"You've been listening to too many ghost stories around the campfire." Starfall stood and patted Sophie's shoulder. "Come on. We only have another half hour or so before we have to get back to camp, and we've only found two cactus. If we're going to make any money, we'd better get busy."

She started to tell Starfall that, if they wanted to make any money, they needed to get lucky, but she kept quiet. After all, it wasn't as if either one of them had hit the jackpot when it came to luck in their lives.

CARMEN HAD BEEN sure that by the next morning she would be over having a man in her house—making a mess in her bathroom, spilling coffee grounds on the counter, pacing her bedroom naked while he was on the phone. Okay, maybe that last part wasn't annoying at all, just incredibly distracting. But, except for the fact that Muffin hissed and headed the other direction anytime Jake came within view, having him around hadn't been a bad thing at all. Was it a haze of sexual attraction making her overlook the disruptions to her calm little world—or was it that part of her recognized she might be overdue for a little disruption?

She was pondering this over the remains of the

omelet Jake had cooked for her (the man had mad kitchen skills—who knew?) when her phone rang. Did mothers have some kind of Mom Radar, that she was calling on this particular morning? "Hi, Mom," Carmen said, prepared to lie and say she was alone if her mother asked. She wasn't ready to be that revealing about her private life.

"We had a really strange visitor here at headquarters," Wilma Redhorse said after she and her daughter had exchanged pleasantries. "Something I thought you might like to know about."

"Oh?" Carmen laid down her fork and looked across the table at Jake, who had picked up on her shift in attitude and was watching her intently. "Who?"

"A Russian man made an appointment with the chairman," Wilma said. "He said he had a business proposition for the tribe. We get that from time to time, especially from Europeans who are looking for new places to invest their money. Most of the time nothing comes of it, but the chairman has a policy that he will hear everyone out."

"What was the business proposition?" Carmen asked.

"He wants to grow cactus. Some kind of rare cactus that other Europeans and Asians will pay a lot of money for. He wanted permission to survey tribal land for the presence of rare species—which I'm thinking means he wants to see how much he can steal out from under our noses." She made a snorting sound. "Not that I'm cynical or anything."

"What was this Russian like?" Carmen asked. "What was his name?"

"He gave me a card. Let's see…his name is Karl Petrov. Big guy—looked a lot like your uncle Ed. As for what he was like—you know the type. Someone whose only knowledge of Native Americans is from bad western movies." She chuckled. "You could tell he was seriously disappointed when the chairman came out of his office and was wearing a suit instead of a loincloth and feathers."

"What did you tell him?" Carmen asked.

"We told him *no*. We don't do joint ventures. We have our own businesses. The chairman also let him know that, if he is caught trespassing on tribal land, he will be arrested and prosecuted. He muttered something in Russian that sounded like curses, but then a lot of foreign languages sound like that to me."

Carmen gripped the phone tightly. "Does his card have any contact information on it?" she asked. "A telephone number or email? Did he mention where he was staying or how to get in touch with him?"

"No. It's just a plain card with his name in English and Russian lettering. We didn't have any desire to talk to him again, so we didn't ask."

"And I guess you didn't get the license plate information on his car? Or security-camera footage that would show that?"

"We don't have security cameras. And why would

we get his plate number?" Wilma said. "What is going on here?"

"That man is wanted for the murder of a federal Fish and Wildlife officer," Carmen said. "If he comes back there, please contact the police and one of us right away. Don't try to hold him yourself, just call us. He's very dangerous."

"All right, dear. But I don't think he's going to come back. The chairman can be pretty fierce when he wants to be, even without a war bonnet."

She hung up the phone. "Karol Petrovsky was at Ute tribal headquarters," she told Jake before he could ask. "He wanted to look for cactus on tribal lands."

"So maybe he is trying to cut out Werner and handle all the business himself," Jake said.

She tucked the phone back into the pocket of her jeans. "I don't like the idea of that killer being so close to my mother."

"Is there any reason to think he'll come back?" Jake asked.

"No. And he didn't leave any contact information. He was using the name Karl Petrov, but I'm sure it was the same man."

"I'll let people know to be on the lookout for that alias. Do you want to go out there and talk to your mother?"

She nodded. "I should interview her and our tribal council chairman to find out what else they can tell us." But more than that, she needed to see for herself that her mother was all right.

"Do you want me to go with you?" he asked.

She shook her head. "You stay and work on things from this end. I'll go by myself." The time with family would do her good, help clear her head of Jake for a while and allow her to think about how she really felt about him—and where she wanted those feelings to take her.

CARMEN WORE HER uniform when she went back to the reservation to interview her mother and the chairman. She needed that symbol of authority to remind her that she was in control. A killer was out there, but she and the other officers hunting for him were going to find him and stop him. And the uniform helped her be in better control of herself and others on the reservation as well. In uniform, she wasn't Wilma and Jim Redhorse's daughter, she was an officer of the law.

She had arranged to meet her mother and the chairman in the tribal council offices, but Rodney Tonaho greeted her when she entered council chambers. "I wanted to get your take on what we're dealing with with this guy," he said. "In case he comes back."

"I doubt he'll come back but, if he does, don't confront him," she said. She looked over her shoulder in time to see her mother and the chairman, Greg Fossey, emerge from the chairman's office. "I want to know exactly what he said to you," she said, hurrying to her mother. "Did he threaten you in any way?"

Wilma waved away her daughter's concern. "He was very polite and respectful," she said. "Persistent, but I admire that in a person."

"He didn't want to take *no* for an answer." Chairman Fossey took Carmen's hand. "It is good to see you again," he said.

"Has the Fish and Wildlife man moved on?" Wilma asked.

"He's still working on the case in Montrose," Carmen said, though she suspected that was not the question her mother had really been asking.

"Why don't we sit down and talk?" Wilma pulled out a chair at the meeting table. "Carmen, you can sit next to Rodney there."

Ignoring her, Carmen took the chair next to her mother. For the next half hour, she went over everything they could tell her about Karl Petrov/Karol Petrovsky. Her mother and the chairman were good at supplying details, but none of it added up to anything that could really help her figure out where Petrovsky was now or what his next move might be.

"We'll keep an eye out for him," Rodney said, standing. "I'll put a deputy on patrol in the area he was interested in, in case he tries to sneak back in."

"Thanks." Carmen stood and shook his hand. "That could be very helpful." She shouldn't let her distaste for her mother's matchmaking get in the way of accepting help from a fellow law enforcement officer. "I'll let you know what we find out."

Rodney left, and the chairman excused himself for another meeting, leaving Wilma alone with her daughter. "That was smart, telling Rodney you'd let him know what happens," she said. "It will give you an excuse to see him again."

Carmen sat back down and faced her mother. "Mom, I'd like you to listen to me," she said.

Wilma widened her eyes. "I always listen to you."

"Then pay special attention now, and remember. I am not interested in Rodney. Not romantically."

Wilma pressed her lips together, then opened them to speak, but Carmen cut her off. "I have a job I love, and I'm not interested in working for the tribal police. I love to come back to the reservation to visit—but not to live."

"You say that now, but you could change your mind," Wilma said.

"I don't think I will but, if I do, it won't be because you keep pressuring me. That isn't going to work."

"I'm not pressuring you. I would never do that."

Wilma's expression showed sufficient outrage that Carmen believed her. Her mother didn't see anything heavy-handed in her attempt to persuade her daughter to move back home and take a job on and marry a man from the reservation. Carmen took her hand and squeezed it. "Mom, I'm not going to leave you. Just because I don't live down the street doesn't mean I'm not just a phone call away. But I need to choose my own place to live and my own job, and I need to choose my own man."

Wilma squeezed her hand, hard enough that it hurt, but Carmen didn't pull away. "Who is the man?" she asked.

Carmen blinked. "What makes you think there's a man?" she asked.

"You're my daughter. I know you. There's something different about you lately. Less…tense. Happier. Connie saw it, too. She called me right after you left here yesterday."

Aunt Connie, who thought she could "see" things about people. Carmen swallowed. "I've been seeing Jake. I like him. A lot."

Wilma nodded. "He has a very strong personality. Maybe that's what you need. It probably doesn't hurt that he's good-looking."

"Mom!" Carmen didn't know whether to be horrified or amused.

"I'm your mother—I'm not dead."

"You're not going to lecture me about marrying someone in the tribe?" Carmen asked.

"Are you going to marry this man—Jake?"

Carmen couldn't keep the heated flush from her face. "I… I don't know." She was a little afraid of how much the idea appealed to her.

"Of course it would be ideal if you married another Ute. But, over the years, it's not as if there hasn't been plenty of marrying outside the tribe. Connie's husband is white, and Veronica's is Mexican, and they're both good men." She took her hand from Carmen's and cupped her daughter's cheeks. "I want you to be happy. And yes—I want to keep you close. I'd hate it if this Jake took you back to Texas or wherever he's from, but it probably wouldn't kill me."

"I don't know what's going to happen, Mom," Carmen said. "But you don't have to worry about me. I want to be happy, too."

"Good. We both want the same thing." Wilma gave Carmen's cheek a little pat, then sat back. "Rodney is going to be disappointed," she said.

"Rodney could have his pick of half the women on the reservation," Carmen said. "Maybe if he knows I'm not available, he'll open his eyes and notice some of them."

"Maybe he will. In the meantime, what about Jake?"

"We're taking things slow." She stood. "I'll let you know. But first, I have to catch a killer."

Chapter Fifteen

"Do you think this dress is all right? Maybe I should change." Phoenix tried to fluff up her limp hair with shaking hands.

Sophie grabbed her mother's wrist and clasped her hand. "You look beautiful, Mom. It'll be okay."

"I don't like doctors," Phoenix said for probably the tenth time since Jake had sent word yesterday that he and Carmen were coming to take her to the clinic the next morning. "I never understand what they're saying, and they rush over my questions."

"Maybe this doctor won't be like that," Sophie said. "And Jake and Carmen will be there with you. They'll make sure your questions get answered." At least, this was what Sophie hoped would happen. She hadn't been to a doctor since a school physical years ago that her grandparents had taken her to. That visit hadn't been so bad. The woman doctor had been friendly, even, and afterwards her grandparents had taken her for ice cream. "Maybe after the visit you can go for ice cream or something," she added.

A knock on the door interrupted before Phoenix could respond to this suggestion. "They're here." She fluttered her hands. "I'm not ready."

Sophie opened the door. Jake's smile made her feel a lot less nervous about this morning—she hoped it did the same for their mom. Jake was so strong and solid and steady. She believed him when he said he was going to take care of them. After all, he had fought the enemy overseas when he was a soldier, and he worked now to fight bad guys as a law enforcement officer. He wasn't about to let anything bad happen to his mom and sister.

"Are you ready to go, Mom?" he asked.

"You look very nice," Carmen said, and Phoenix gave her a grateful smile.

"I'm not ready," Phoenix said again. She smoothed her skirt. "But I'm going to go anyway."

Jake turned to Sophie. "We shouldn't be too long," he said. "You'll be all right here on your own?"

Sophie stared at him. "I'm going with you," she said.

"No!" Phoenix's voice rose. "I don't want you there, Sophie. You stay here where I'll know you're safe."

"Why wouldn't I be safe with you and Jake and Carmen?" Sophie frowned at her mother. "I want to go with you."

"I think it would be smart if you stayed here," Jake said. "Especially if it makes Mom feel better to know you're here."

"But I want to go!" She knew she sounded like a whiny little kid, but how could they possibly think it was right to leave her out of this? "I want to hear what the doctor has to say to Mom."

Carmen put a hand on her shoulder. "I promise I'll tell you everything he said." She met Sophie's gaze and held it. "I promise."

She started to protest again, but a look from Jake silenced her. "I promise to bring you a treat when I come back," Phoenix said.

"I'm not a baby," Sophie said. "You don't have to bribe me."

Hurt filled Phoenix's watery blue eyes. "You'll always be my baby," she said.

Sophie turned away. She couldn't believe after all the time she had spent worrying about her mother and taking care of her when she didn't feel well, they were going to leave her behind. She would have to rely on them to tell her what they thought she ought to know about her mom's medical condition—which wouldn't necessarily be everything the doctor said. So she wasn't going to pretend she was happy about any of it.

She stayed inside the trailer until she was sure they were gone, then she left and headed to Starfall's tent. "Do you want to go hunt cactus this morning?" she asked when Starfall answered her knock on the tent pole.

"I thought you were going to the doctor with your mother and brother," Starfall said.

"Yeah, I decided not to go." The lie was easier than telling the truth. The last thing she wanted was for Starfall to feel sorry for her or anything. "I'd rather stay here and make some money."

"I like the way you think." Starfall said. "Give me a minute, and I'll be out."

Five minutes later, she emerged from the tent with Hunter in a sling. "If he gets fussy, maybe you can carry him for a while," she said. "He likes you." She handed Sophie her backpack. "You can carry this."

The day was bright but breezy. The wind was cool and carried the scents of sage and creosote—the perfume of the high desert, Sophie thought. She would miss that smell if she and Mom went to live someplace else with Jake. But there would probably be good smells there, too. Pine trees or flowers and things like that. Or maybe cars and smog if they went to live in a city. Still, she hoped they could live in the country or a small town. Mom didn't like cities—and cities might make it easier to fall into her old life, with drugs and the wrong kind of friends. But she might be happy in the country, with flowers and a garden to tend.

Starfall led the way across the prairie, away from the ravine where they had picked berries to a plateau, where the wind had carved sandstone into towers and arches, and big boulders looked like fantastic sculptures that sparkled with glittery pyrite and quartz. "Is this where Jake was camped?" Sophie asked.

"Somewhere in here." Starfall adjusted Hunter

in his sling. "I guess he's in town now. Or shacked up with Carmen."

Sophie wasn't about to speculate on that, so she slipped off the heavy backpack and started searching the ground for cactus. She found lots of wildflowers and weeds, and spotted a couple of horned toads, which looked like miniature triceratops crouched in the dried grass, staring up at her with shining eyes. Why was it so hard to find those little cactus? Then again, if they were easy to locate, they probably wouldn't be worth twenty dollars each to the German.

"When are you supposed to meet with that German guy again?" she asked as she and Starfall searched around the rocks.

"I told him I would have some cactus for him tomorrow," Starfall said. "He promised to bring the money, so we need to fill up that backpack."

"Maybe Jake was wrong about there being any around here," Sophie said. "I haven't seen—wait." She knelt, and a thrill of excitement bubbled up through her. "Wow—there's three of them right here!"

"Then, get digging." Starfall handed her a trowel, and Sophie carefully dug around the little spiny balls.

"I can't believe people collect these," she said as she loosened first one cactus, then a second. "I can think of a lot better things to spend money on." If she had a lot of money, she would buy lots of books—and a puppy. She had always wanted a puppy, but they had never lived anywhere she could have one. Maybe Jake would let her have a dog when they moved in with him…

A scream tore at the morning stillness, high and piercing. Sophie dropped the trowel and spun around to stare at Starfall. She stood a few yards away, clutching Hunter to her chest and staring at a big man who had a big gun trained on her.

The man swung the gun to point at Sophie. It was a handgun, but the barrel was long, and the opening looked to Sophie as big around as a half-dollar. "What do you think you're doing, scaring us this way?" she yelped. Maybe it wasn't the smartest thing to say to a guy with a gun, but Sophie couldn't think of anything else to say.

"I need you to come with me," the man said. He spoke good English, but with a heavy accent. Russian, maybe?

"What are you going to do with us?" Sophie asked.

"Get up!" the man shouted.

Sophie stood. Starfall was frozen in place. She must have been squeezing Hunter too tight because he began to wail, the sound setting Sophie's teeth on edge. She stared at the man. He didn't look friendly, and she didn't think he had anything pleasant in mind. Her stomach heaved at the idea, but she tried to ignore the sick feeling.

"Quiet!" he barked. Starfall flinched, but Hunter kept wailing.

"You scared him," Sophie said, drawing the man's

attention once more. That was what she had to do, she saw now. She needed to distract the man and give Starfall a chance to get away. She could protect Hunter and go for help at the same time. She could drive to town and get Jake. Sophie would be all right until he came for her. "What are you doing out here, scaring people?" she asked the man.

He kept looking at her. She put her hand behind her back and made a shooing motion she hoped Starfall would notice. *Get out of here while you can*, she thought, trying to telegraph the words to Starfall. *Take Hunter, and run!*

"What are you doing out here?" the man asked.

The question surprised Sophie. She had been expecting another order. "We're looking for cactus." She held out her hand, one of the little cactus balanced on her palm. "Do you want to see?"

The man didn't come any closer, but he kept his eyes on Sophie. "You work for Werner, don't you?" he said.

"I'm collecting cactus to sell," Sophie said. "I don't care who I sell them to. If you want to pay me for them, I'll sell them to you." She didn't look toward Starfall and Hunter. She kept her eyes locked on the man's, making sure he didn't look over in that direction, either. "I have more here, if you want to see them." She reached to pull off the backpack, but the man jutted the gun at her. "Don't move."

Sophie held out both hands. "Okay, okay. Do you want to look or not?"

"Turn around," the man ordered.

Sophie turned, still avoiding looking toward the rocks. She hoped Starfall wasn't standing there like a statue. At least Hunter had stopped wailing. The man approached, focused, as Sophie had hoped, on the cactus. He opened the backpack and looked inside.

Then he shoved hard. Sophie landed on her hands and knees in the dirt and rocks. "Ouch!" she wailed, maybe a little louder than necessary. "What did you do that for?" She looked over her shoulder at the man.

"There are only two cactus in there," he said. "I need more than that. Many more."

"You interrupted me before I had been hunting very long," she said. "If you give me time, I can find more for you."

"I have other things in mind for you." He motioned with the gun. "Get up."

Sophie stood and brushed off her knees, which stung from their impact with the hard ground. "Where are you taking me?" she asked.

But the man didn't answer. He had turned toward where Starfall and Hunter had been standing—except now there were only piles of rock. Starfall was gone. Now Sophie was alone with the big man and more afraid than she had ever been in her life.

CARMEN HAD VOLUNTEERED one summer at the tribal clinic where her aunt worked—or rather, her mother had signed her up for the job, then told Carmen it was her duty to help out. She had spent most of her time escorting elderly men and women into the exam rooms, filing charts and cleaning up rooms between patient visits. Not difficult work, but not very exciting, either. And while her aunt had tried to interest her in assisting with blood draws and learning how to bandage wounds, Carmen had decided very quickly that she wanted nothing to do with the messy, bloody side of medicine.

So she couldn't say she was completely comfortable with the idea of escorting Jake and his mom to Phoenix's appointment at the Montrose clinic. But however ill at ease she felt, it was nothing compared to the grim expression on Jake's face and the look of abject terror in Phoenix's eyes. As the three of them walked into the clinic, Phoenix took hold of Carmen's hand and refused to let go.

Jake let the receptionist know they were there, then settled into a chair that looked too small for him, hands gripping the arms white-knuckled. Carmen wanted to swat his arm and tell him he wasn't helping his mother by looking as if he was waiting for his turn in the torture chamber. "My aunt's clinic is a lot like this," Carmen said, trying to sound a lot more cheerful than she felt. "She's been working there so long she knows the name of everyone who comes in the door. Sometimes it's more like a reunion than a doctor's visit, what with everyone catching up on each other's news."

"I want you to go into the room with me," Phoenix said. She still had a death grip on Carmen's hand.

"Oh. Well, I—" Carmen shot a desperate look to Jake. "Wouldn't you rather Jake—?"

"He can't go in with me." Phoenix was clearly horrified at the idea.

"I can't go in with her," Jake agreed.

Okay. Maybe Carmen could see her point. What woman wanted to wear one of those drafty gowns in front of her grown son? "All right," she said. "I'll go with you."

They didn't have to wait long. A woman in purple scrubs called for Phoenix. She stood, tugging Carmen up alongside her, and they followed the nurse or tech or whatever she was into an exam room.

Phoenix didn't let go of Carmen's hand until the woman in scrubs asked her to sit on the paper-covered table. Carmen took the only other seat in the room, a folding chair in the corner, and studied the artwork on the walls, while Phoenix submitted to having her blood pressure and temperature checked.

"Sophie wasn't too happy about being left at home," Phoenix said, when she and Carmen were alone again.

"She's worried about you," Carmen said. "She'll be fine by the time you get back to camp."

"She worries too much," Phoenix said. "I shouldn't have put her in that position. She's still just a kid. She should be focused on kid problems, not adult ones."

"She's very mature for her age," Carmen said.

Phoenix slumped, perched on the edge of the table, feet dangling. "I did that to Jake, too," she said. "He had to practically raise himself, I was so caught up in my own problems. But I've tried to be a better mother to Sophie."

"Jake turned out all right," Carmen said. More than all right, if things had been as rough as he had hinted at. "And he loves you and Sophie very much."

Phoenix sniffed. "He does, doesn't he? I don't really deserve it, I guess, but he does."

"Of course you deserve it," Carmen said. "You did the best you could."

"But sometimes my best wasn't very good at all." She plucked at the edge of her blouse—they hadn't asked her to change into a gown after all. "I don't want to leave the camp. I know it's hard for him to understand, but I like it there. I feel safe."

"Jake would do his best to keep you safe wherever you went with him," Carmen said. "And if you need more medical care, it would be easier to get in a town. And Sophie could go to school and have friends her own age."

Phoenix sighed. "That's what Jake says. I don't know. I've never set a lot of importance on doing things just because they were easy or what other people thought was normal."

Carmen was saved from having to make a reply by the entrance of the doctor, an efficient, middle-aged woman who introduced herself, then conducted what seemed to Carmen's eyes to be a thorough exam. After several minutes of probing and asking questions, she stepped back. "The first step is to do some blood work," she said. "I wouldn't be surprised if you're a little anemic, and we might spot some other insufficiencies, but we'll wait until we get the results back in a day or two and address those." She patted Phoenix's arms. "After we draw your blood, I want you to go back home and rest, and try not to worry."

Phoenix sat up straighter, a little color in her cheeks. "You're not going to put me in the hospital?" she asked.

"I don't see any need for that," the doctor said. "Do you want to go to the hospital?"

"No!" Phoenix shook her head. "I want to go home to my daughter."

"You do that, and I'll be in touch with a plan once I see the blood work."

"Thank you," Phoenix said. She turned to Carmen. "I can go home."

Carmen hugged her. "That's great news."

A medical assistant came in and drew Phoenix's blood, then Carmen walked with the older woman to the waiting room. Jake stood to meet them "Well?" he asked.

"She drew some blood, and she told me to go home and rest," Phoenix said as she moved past him toward the door.

"But what did the doctor say?" He followed his

mother and Carmen into the parking lot. "What does she think is wrong?"

"I might be anemic. It might be something else." Phoenix grabbed the door handle of the truck. "Unlock this so we can go home."

Jake unlocked the truck and hurried around to the driver's side. "That's it?" He looked to Carmen for confirmation.

"That's about it," Carmen said. She slid into the passenger seat, with Phoenix between her and Jake. "She'll know more when she gets the results of the blood tests."

"Okay." He sagged back against the seat. "So now I guess we wait."

"Now we go home." Phoenix prodded him with her elbow. "Start the truck, and let's go."

He turned the key in the ignition. "Do you want to go somewhere for lunch or something first?" he asked.

"No. I want to go home."

Jake looked across at Carmen and shrugged, then put the truck in gear and backed out of his parking space. No one said much on the way back to camp. Carmen thought Phoenix might have nodded off. Poor thing probably hadn't slept much last night.

The ring of Jake's phone was jarring in the silence. He hit the button to answer the call. "This is Jake."

"It's Marco at Ranger headquarters." Marco Cruz said. "Can you head this way?"

"What's up?" Jake asked.

"Starfall just showed up here in a panic. She says some Russian guy has your sister."

Chapter Sixteen

Cars filled the parking lot at Ranger headquarters. Jake even spotted a TV-news van. "How did the media get wind of this already?" Carmen asked, as Jake slid into a spot at the back of the lot. He had his door open before the engine had even fallen silent. Carmen was right behind him, one arm around Phoenix, who looked as if she might collapse any minute. Carmen hadn't said much since Marco's call, but her presence steadied Jake. She wasn't freaking out about this, so neither would he.

At least a dozen people waited at headquarters, and everyone seemed to be talking at once. At Jake's entrance, the noise level dropped. Marco hurried to him. "Starfall is back here," he said, gestioning toward the conference room. "I'll let her tel. happened."

Starfall sat at the conference table, i. officers Ethan Reynolds and Simon Woolri. cradled her baby, murmuring softly to him. When Carmen, Phoenix and Jake stepped into the room.

she rose. "I wouldn't have left her with him if I had had any other choice," she said. "I had to go for help. You see that, don't you?"

The idea that she had left Sophie—a child—at the mercy of a strange man made Jake's vision cloud. He took a deep breath, fighting for control. He couldn't help Sophie unless he stayed calm. "Tell me what happened," he said and sat in the chair across from her.

Starfall's gaze shifted to Carmen, who was settling Phoenix in the chair next to Jake, and her bottom lip trembled, but she sat and made an effort to control her emotions. "Sophie came to me this morning, after you left to take Phoenix to the doctor. She asked if we could go look for cactus."

"We should have taken her with us," Phoenix said. "She wanted to go and, if we hadn't left her in camp, this wouldn't have happened."

"This is the kidnapper's fault, not yours," Jake said. He turned back to Starfall. "Why did she want to look for cactus?"

"I promised her ten dollars—half of what Werner said he would pay me—for every cactus she found," Starfall said. "She wanted to earn money to help pay Phoenix's medical bills."

Phoenix broke down sobbing. Carmen comforted her. Maybe Jake should have been the one to try to calm her, but Sophie needed him more now. "I told her I'd pay for everything," he said. "She didn't have to worry about that."

"I don't know anything about that," Starfall said. "Anyway, we set out. I was carrying Hunter and Sophie had my backpack. We headed toward the area where you were camped before. I remembered you said you saw some of those cactus there."

Jake glanced at Ethan and Simon. "I don't know what the area is called, but I can show you on a map," he said.

Simon nodded. "We'll get Randall and his dog out there. If Lotte can pick up a scent, she might be able to lead us to him."

"You don't even know what you're looking for yet," Starfall said. "Do you want me to finish my story or not?"

"Go ahead," Jake said.

She settled back in her chair. "Sophie found some of the cactus and was digging them up, when this big guy steps out from behind a rock and points this huge gun at us. He had a Russian accent, and he told us if we tried anything, he would kill us. I think he would have, too."

"How do you know the accent was Russian?" Simon asked.

"Because it was. I mean, it wasn't German like Werner's, or French or Spanish. It was Russian." She looked to Jake again. "He was really big—over six feet, with broad shoulders. But he had a gut on him, too."

"How old was he?" Ethan asked.

She wrinkled her nose. "Maybe fifty? Not young. He was really solid."

"What did he say?" Jake asked. "What did he want with you?"

"He asked about the cactus. Sophie told him we were collecting them to sell to Werner, but he could have them if he wanted. I thought maybe we could make a deal and he'd let us go, but that didn't work."

"How did you get away?" Carmen asked.

"Sophie started talking to him, keeping his attention on her. But she motioned to me behind her back. I was so frightened it took me a little bit to realize she was motioning for me to run away. I didn't want to leave her, but I had my baby to think of and, if I got away, I knew I could get help."

"What did you do?" Carmen asked.

"At first, I ducked behind the rock. When he didn't react, I started moving away, going from rock to tree, trying to hide. Every second I kept expecting him to shoot me in the back. But he never did. When I was far enough away that I was sure he couldn't see me, I took off running. I ran to camp, got my car and came here."

"You did the right thing," Carmen said. She looked at Jake when she said the words, and he nodded. If Starfall hadn't run when she had the chance, Jake probably still wouldn't know that Sophie was missing. The Russian would have an even bigger head start.

"What did this Russian say he wanted with you and Sophie?" he asked.

"He didn't," Starfall said. "He just said he had plans for us." Her eyes shone with tears. "You don't think he'll hurt her, do you? She's just a girl. A very brave girl."

"Jake, what are you going to do?" Phoenix clutched at his arm. "You can't let him hurt her."

Jake leaned across the table, his eyes locked on Starfall's. "Did this Russian have a car? Did you see one anywhere nearby?"

She shook her head. "All I saw was the gun. And a backpack!" She sat up straighter. "He was wearing a backpack. The big kind, like campers use, with a bedroll and other stuff tied on it. Does that help?"

Jake nodded. "Werner said the Russian was camping. If he had to hike a ways to get to a car, that would slow him down. We might even get lucky, and he's still in the area."

"Then you can find her," Phoenix said. "She'll be all right."

He patted his mother's arm. "That's the plan." No point mentioning that Sophie and her captor might be anywhere in the thousands of acres of wilderness in the area. Finding them wasn't as simple as heading to the nearest campground.

A commotion outside the conference room distracted him. Marco was already moving toward the door when it burst open, and Daniel Metwater stumbled in. "I came as soon as I heard," he said.

Phoenix rose. "I should have known you'd be concerned about one of your disciples," she said.

Metwater ignored her and turned to Jake. "I told you the Russian mafia was after me," he said. "Why wouldn't you listen? You've got to stop him, or I'll be next."

"Why do you think this has anything to do with you?" Jake asked.

"Isn't it obvious? They knew Sophie was special to me, so they took her. It's the way they do things—they want to send me a warning. To make me afraid."

Jake hadn't even realized he had made a fist and had his arm drawn back, ready to punch Metwater, when Carmen took hold of his arm. "He's not worth it," she said softly.

Jake studied the so-called Prophet, his hair a tangle, his shirt half-unbuttoned. He was so focused on himself, he couldn't even find concern for a child who had been kidnapped. But he might be useful to them after all. "Have you had any other 'messages' from the Russian?" he asked. "Any communications at all—letters, visits?"

Metwater shook his head.

"What about Werner Altbusser?" Carmen asked. "Have you talked to him since he was in your camp the day before yesterday?"

Metwater flicked his gaze to her. "Werner has nothing to do with this," he said.

"Maybe he and the Russian are working together," Starfall said.

Everyone turned to stare at her. "It makes sense," she continued. "Werner didn't want to pay me for the cactus, so he sent the Russian to collect them."

"But you offered to give them to the Russian, didn't you?" Jake asked. "Why bother kidnapping Sophie?"

"She told him we would sell him the cactus," Starfall said. "Of course, since he had the gun, we would have had to give them to him. Werner would have known that—the big cheat."

"I told you, he took Sophie because of me," Metwater said. "Why are you standing here wasting time? You have to go after him."

"We're getting together a search party to go out now," Marco told Jake. "Do you and Carmen want to come?"

"I'll catch up with you in a little while. I have something else to do first." Jake turned to Carmen. "Can you take Mom back to the camp for me?"

"Of course." Carmen looked into his eyes, searching. "What are you going to do?"

"I'm going to see Werner. He knows this Russian better than any of us. He might have an idea where he's camping."

"That's a good idea," she said. "Do you want me to go with you?"

He shook his head. "I need you to look after Mom. And I know Sophie trusts you. In case they find her before I get back, I'd like you there with her."

"All right." She gripped his hand. "Be careful."

"I will." But he wasn't going to leave Werner until he knew everything the German could tell him about his Russian "friend."

SOPHIE TRUDGED ALONG in the hot sun, her gaze focused on the broad back of her captor. When he had discovered Starfall had run away, he had yelled a lot—some in English, and some in what she guessed was Russian. Sophie watched him rant and didn't say anything. He waved the gun at her a lot, but he never actually shot it. She knew that he could—that he might shoot her still. But for now, he had only tied her up, then tied one end of the rope around his waist and led her off across the wilderness. He muttered a lot under his breath—words she couldn't understand—and, every so often, he glared at her over his shoulder and tugged on the rope to make her go faster, as if she was a dog.

"Where are you taking me?" she asked.

He didn't answer.

"Who are you?" she asked. "What do you want with me?"

Still no answer. Her gaze shifted to Starfall's backpack, which he had tied to his own pack. "I can find some more of those cactus for you, if you want," she said.

He still didn't say anything, but his head came up, and she could tell he was listening. "Why are people so interested in those little cactus, anyway?" she asked. "I wouldn't pay a quarter for one."

"Everything is worth what people will pay for it," the Russian said. "People will pay a lot of money for all kinds of cactus. I have made much money over the years, selling them what they want."

"What does any of that have to do with me?" Sophie asked.

The icy look he gave her made her want to throw up. "Some people will pay money for girls, too," he said. "You do what I tell you, or I might decide to sell you to one of them."

She swallowed hard. "Is that why you kidnapped me? To s-sell me?"

He kicked a rock, sending it careering and bouncing across the rough ground. "Why can't you be quiet?"

She stuck her chin out. She wouldn't let him see she was afraid. "Because I want to know. Why can't you just tell me?"

He lunged back toward her. She tried not to flinch, but she couldn't help it. "Do you know how to make someone do what you want them to do?" he growled.

"H-how?"

"You take something of theirs. It causes more pain than if you broke their knees or cut off their hand. If you choose the right thing to take—the right person—then you will have them completely under your power."

His words made her feel cold all over. "Who are you trying to control?" she asked. If he said *Met-*

water, she would scream. She wasn't his, no matter what anyone else said.

The Russian narrowed his eyes. "Don't pretend to be stupid, when I can see you are not. Your brother is a federal agent who has been following that idiot, Werner. Werner is too stupid to recognize him for what he is, but I can spot the police from two blocks away."

"What do you want from my brother?" she asked.

"I want him to go away. Tell his superiors he knows nothing about me. He can arrest Werner if he likes, that useless cheat. He thought I was so stupid I couldn't see he was keeping most of the profits from the cactus for himself, even though I did all of the work of finding the buyers and selling to them. I took all the risk, yet he expected me to be happy with the scraps he threw to me." He spat in the dirt.

"If Werner is the one you're mad at, why not kidnap him?" Sophie asked.

"Because he could still be useful to me. He is trying to make a deal with the leader of that commune you live in—that so-called Prophet. He wants this 'Prophet' to tell all his followers to collect the cactus for Werner. If they agree to this arrangement, I can step in and take over. Then maybe I will get rid of him."

"Did you kill Reggae?" she asked. Her throat hurt, thinking about the dead man. He had always been friendly to her, and the way he tried so hard to get

Starfall to notice him was kind of sweet. "Why? He never hurt anyone."

"I wanted Werner to know that I meant business by going after one of his workers. If he didn't turn everything over to me, I would kill everyone close to him, until he was all alone. And, finally, I would come for him." He smiled an awful, cold expression that made Sophie's stomach hurt.

He straightened and glared down at her. "Your brother will come after you, no?"

She nodded. Of course Jake would come after her.

"You'd better hope he does," the Russian said. "If he doesn't, I will kill you. Even if you are a smart girl."

JAKE SPED INTO the lot of the motel, parked behind Werner's rented SUV, blocking it in, and stormed up to the door of Werner's room. He pounded on the door, rattling it in its frame. "Open up, Werner! If you don't, I swear I'll kick the door in."

"Who...who is it?" The German's voice quavered.

"Someone you don't want to cross," Jake said.

The chain rattled, and the door eased open. Jake grabbed the German by the throat and shoved him back into the room, kicking the door closed behind him. He forced Werner's back against the wall. "Tell me where the Russian is camping. Your 'friend,' Karol Petrovsky."

Werner's pupils dilated, and his skin was the color

of mashed potatoes. "I... I don't know what you're talking about."

"Don't lie to me!" Jake tightened his hold. "He has my sister, and I need to know how to find him."

Werner muttered something in German that might have been a prayer. "Where is he?" Jake demanded.

"I don't know for sure. I only suspect."

Jake released his hold on Werner and shoved him onto the bed. "What do you suspect?"

Werner rubbed his neck. "Why do you think I know where he is?"

"That day I caught you in my camp—you were looking for him, weren't you?"

Werner's face drooped, making him look much older, and he nodded. "A mutual acquaintance had told me he was in the area."

"What is he to you? Your friend? Your partner?" Jake shoved his hands in his pockets. He couldn't let his temper and his worry over Sophie get the best of him. He had a job to do, and that meant keeping his cool.

"Not my friend!" Werner shook his head, adamant. "We were partners at one time—business partners."

"But you aren't now?"

"No. We had a disagreement over how profits should be divided."

"When was the last time you talked to him?"

"Months ago. Six months ago. I don't want to talk to him. Not ever again."

"Yet you were looking for his camp that day."

"Yes. But that was before he killed that young man. And then he killed the man who was in the room next door." He pointed to his left.

"How do you know it was him?" Jake asked.

Werner looked away.

Jake took his hands from his pockets and leaned toward him. "Tell me."

"I saw him. I looked out the window and saw him. I thought he was coming for me. To kill me. But he went into the room next door instead."

"Why? Why would he kill that man instead of you? Why would he kill that kid?"

"He must have seen me talking to them. He thought they were working for me. That is how they do things, these Russians that he associates with. They attack people close to you first, to send a warning. They want to make you so afraid that, by the time they get to you, you will do anything they ask."

"What does Petrovsky want from you?"

"He wants to take over my business."

"What business is that?"

Again, Werner's gaze shifted away. "It does not matter."

"It does matter." Jake leaned toward him again so that the German leaned back on the bed. "You're illegally exporting cactus from the United States to Europe, including a number of endangered species."

"They are only little cactus," Werner protested.

"And there are so many of them. What difference does it make to you?"

"Then you admit that's what you've been doing here?" Jake said. "You were paying people like the young man who was killed to collect the cactus for you?"

"What if I was? Who are you to care?"

Jake pulled his credentials from his pocket. "Officer Jacob Lohmiller, US Fish and Wildlife." He shoved the wallet back into his pocket and took out a pair of flex cuffs and grabbed Werner's wrist. "Werner Altbusser, you're under arrest." He recited Werner's rights and confirmed that Werner understood them.

Jake braced himself for a struggle, but the German merely slumped onto the bed again. "I am ruined," he said. "I was ruined before you came here. Karol is taking my business. I will be lucky if he doesn't take my life."

"Tell me where to find him, and I'll lock him up, too," Jake said as he fastened the cuffs. "If you get lucky, you can work a deal to testify against him."

This idea seemed to bolster the German's spirits. "I will tell you what I know," he said. "But I don't know if it will be any help. Who did you say he has taken?"

"My sister. She's fourteen years old."

Werner's eyes widened. "That is bad. Very bad."

"Tell me where he is. Where is his camp? Is it

near where I was camping? Is that why you were looking there?"

Werner shook his head. "I never found it, but I was looking there because last year he insisted I bring him with me on my collecting trip to the United States, and that is the area where we camped. I thought he would go back there because it was familiar to him."

"Come on." He pulled Werner with him toward the door.

"What are you doing? Where are you taking me?"

"You're going with me to find Sophie."

"But I told you—I don't know where Karol is."

"Then you had better hope you get lucky."

Chapter Seventeen

"Tell me again where you were when you and Sophie were taken." Carmen put her face very close to Starfall's. She could smell the tomatoes the other woman had had for lunch and the coppery tang of sweat and fear. "Exactly where you were."

"I don't remember exactly." Starfall looked over Carmen's shoulder, at the other searchers who had assembled outside of Metwater's camp to look for Sophie. Carmen had given Starfall a ride back to camp with her and Phoenix. "We were somewhere near where Jake was camped," Starfall said. "There were a bunch of big rocks. And some of those cactus we were looking for."

Carmen suppressed a groan of frustration.

"This place is crawling with rocks and cactus," Simon, who was standing behind her, said. "And Jake isn't here to ask where he was camping. Why is that?"

"He went to talk someone who knows the man who took Sophie," Carmen said.

"Who probably isn't going to tell him anything," Simon said.

"I don't know about that," Evan said. "Something tells me Jake can be pretty persuasive when he wants to be."

"You have to find her." Phoenix stood with Daniel Metwater and some of the other women at the edge of the parking area where the searchers had assembled.

Simon turned toward Phoenix, but Carmen answered first. "We're going to find her," she said, with more conviction in her voice than she really felt. The Russian had already left two dead men in his wake. Why would he want to be burdened with a fourteen-year-old girl?

"Let's get going!" Simon directed the searchers, who planned to cover the area in a grid pattern. Carmen stayed back in case Phoenix needed her. Starfall put a hand on her arm.

"I just remembered something," Starfall said.

Carmen waited, saying nothing.

"We were really near that place where we were all picking berries the first day Jake came into camp with you," Starfall said. "There's this high point there that kind of overlooks the whole area. The Russian must have been hiding up there, watching us."

Carmen felt a rush of recognition. She had a clear picture of Jake lying prone, field glasses focused on the little group of women and the girl, while she circled around to confront him, the first day they had met. He had chosen the perfect vantage point to surveil them—something the Russian must have realized as well. "Can you stay here with Phoenix?" she asked.

Starfall nodded. "Of course."

"Thanks." Carmen hurried to catch up with the searchers. They had set out fast and were already some distance ahead, traveling in the wrong direction. She would have to catch up to them, then waste time persuading them that she knew the spot where they should look.

She turned away and set out on her own toward Jake's lookout point. He was only one man, with one girl. She was a trained officer, with her weapons, and a personal stake in saving the sister of the man she had fallen in love with. What men might offer in power she would make up for with finesse and determination.

Fifteen minutes of alternately walking and running brought her to the spot Starfall had described. She spotted a small trowel and a half-excavated clump of cactus beside it. The trail was easy to follow from there—two sets of prints in the fine desert dust, broken branches and disturbed rocks. Tracking them was so easy, Carmen knew the man wanted to be followed. He expected he would be found, which meant he would be waiting for her.

But would he expect a woman to come after him? Carmen asked herself. Probably not. Maybe she could use that to her advantage.

She slowed her pace, moving stealthily and keeping to cover. When she spotted the narrow box canyon shielded by a growth of trees, she stopped. The canyon would provide a perfect camp, with shelter from the wind, shade from the worst of the afternoon sun, perhaps fresh water from a spring or creek and, most important, only one way in or out. It was the perfect place to hide—and the perfect place to set a trap.

Instead of approaching the canyon directly, she veered to one side and began climbing up above it, working her way up the increasingly steep slope, stepping carefully to avoid dislodging loose rock. When something burst from the brush to her left, she had her weapon drawn and aimed before she could even process the thought, and stood, panting, heart pounding, her gun aimed at a startled mule deer, a trembling half-grown fawn at its side.

Shaking from the flood of adrenaline, she holstered the gun and watched as the deer ambled away. As soon as her legs felt steady, she set out again.

When the ground leveled out once more, she moved to the canyon's edge and looked down. But trees and rocks blocked her view. If she was going to find the Russian's camp, she would have to move lower.

She climbed down, keeping to the cover of trees and boulders, moving laterally as she descended, so that she moved further and further into the canyon. She estimated she had been traveling perhaps five minutes, when a flash of something pink made her freeze. She held her breath, waiting, and Sophie shuffled into view, her hands and feet shackled.

Three feet behind the girl was the Russian, a long-barreled revolver in his hand. Carmen drew her own weapon and sited in on him. She would need to wait until Sophie wasn't so close to him. Right now, it would be too easy for him to use the girl as a shield or even kill her before Carmen could react.

Sophie sat down on top of a blue and white picnic cooler. The Russian moved past her to a green nylon tent that was almost invisible in the underbrush. With the girl shackled, he had no fear of her running off. He was waiting for the searchers to come to them. Maybe they were why he had taken Sophie in the first place.

Or he wanted to get the attention of one particular searcher.

Daniel Metwater? Carmen shook her head. Though the Prophet was clearly terrified of the Russian, she didn't buy Metwater's story that he was the real target. If that was the case, why not go after Andi Mattheson who, as Asteria, lived with Metwater and was clearly closer to him than a fourteen-year-old girl?

That left Jake. It wouldn't be the first time a criminal had tried to get to a lawman by threatening his family. But this time it wasn't going to work. Carmen tightened her grip on her weapon.

After a glance over her shoulder toward the tent, Sophie stood and moved to the edge of the growth of trees where Carmen hid. She peered intently into the underbrush, and a smile transformed her face when she recognized Carmen. Still perfectly silent, she held out her manacled hands in a pleading gesture.

Carmen frowned. She didn't have anything with her to remove or sever the shackles, which appeared to be made of metal. The Russian had definitely come prepared. They wouldn't be able to run from him with Sophie hampered in that way. Their only hope was for Carmen to subdue him. She would have to catch him off guard and away from Sophie.

She motioned the girl back toward the cooler. Sophie frowned and didn't move. *Go!* Carmen mouthed, but still the girl remained rooted in place.

"What are you doing up?" The Russian's voice was loud, with a heavy accent. Sophie stumbled backwards and almost fell over. The Russian moved in behind her and took her arm, while Carmen retreated further into the underbrush. She didn't dare try for him now, not with his hands on Sophie.

He led the girl back to the cooler and shoved her down once more. Sophie kept looking toward Carmen. *Don't look at me*, Carmen silently pleaded. The Russian would figure out she was here.

She took a step back, thinking it safer to put extra distance between herself and the camp. She didn't see the rock that moved under her feet, rolling down the hill and into the camp, sending her falling with a flailing of arms and a crack of branches.

Seconds later she was staring into the barrel of

that revolver, pointed at her head. "Hello," the Russian said, his tone light, almost conversational. "Drop your weapon, and stand up slowly."

She did as he asked, gaze shifting between his eyes and the gun. Neither offered any comfort. The gun and the eyes were both cold and lethal. He made a grunting noise as she stood. "I recognize you," he said. "You are the girlfriend. The other cop."

She said nothing. What would be the point?

The Russian nodded and motioned her toward the camp. "You could be useful," he said. "If your game-warden friend doesn't respond to his sister's distress to meet my demands, I can cut off your head and send it to him to drive the message home."

WERNER DIRECTED JAKE to the forest service road where Jake had been camped. "We camped along in here last year, but I don't remember exactly where," Werner said.

"Why aren't you camping this year?" Jake asked.

"Camping was Karol's idea," Werner said. "I prefer to stay in hotel. But he likes to pretend he is a pioneer outdoorsman. Plus, he is cheap, and camping like this is free."

They set out walking, searching for some sign of Petrovsky and Sophie—or anyone else. "There was no one else camped here when we were here, either," Werner said. "Karol liked that. It went along with his fantasy of being a wilderness explorer. He has a great fascination with the American West."

"I heard he approached the Southern Ute tribe about raising cactus on their land," Jake said.

"Except collectors don't want farmed cactus," Werner said. "The ones who will pay the most money—collectors in Japan and Germany—they want wild plants. I told you Karol is fascinated by the whole mountain man, cowboys-and-Indians thing. He thinks, because he isn't from the United States, he really understands Native Americans. He thinks they will accept him as one of their own. I tried to tell him he was full of it, but he's crazy. He gets an idea in his head and decides that it's right and there's no talking him out of it."

"What idea made him kidnap my sister?"

Werner looked more woeful than ever. "I am sorry, I do not know. I truly believe he is crazy."

Jake might go crazy if anything happened to Sophie. Werner stopped at a pull-out alongside the road. "We camped in a place very like this, but I don't know that Karol would come back to the same place. It was only a hunch." He looked around them. "I'm sorry. I don't know."

"Let's walk a little farther," Jake said. They were very near where he had camped when he had first come to the area to look for his mother and Sophie. So much had happened since then—he didn't even feel like the same man. He had had a mission then, but the mission had changed to one that was so much more important. He was still on the trail of a smuggler, but his sister's life was at stake. He couldn't make any wrong moves.

He studied the terrain, searching for anything familiar, and tried to put himself in the crazy Russian's head. That's what they had taught him in the military—*think like the enemy.*

Petrovsky would want a good position from which to hold Sophie but also a camp that enabled him to see anyone coming, without being seen himself. He was a fan of cowboys-and-Indians stories. Where had the cowboys always holed up? Jake's store of cowboy lore was painfully small, but hadn't there been something about Butch Cassidy and the Hole-in-the-Wall Gang making their camp in a box canyon? The Russian would like that—only one way in, and he could look out on the world from safety.

Jake pulled out the map they had brought along, spread it out and studied it. After a few minutes, he found what he was looking for. He put his finger over the squiggly line that outlined the box canyon. "That's where I think he is," he said.

"What do we do now?" Werner asked.

Jake folded the map and stuffed it into his pocket. "Come on." He traveled away from the canyon, then circled back to approach it from the side. Behind him, Werner, hands cuffed in front of him, panted and puffed, occasionally stumbling and grunting, but the German made no protest. When they were at the rim of the canyon, Jake stopped. "Sit here and don't make a sound while I check things out," he said.

Werner's face drooped. "At least remove the cuffs," he said. "I will do whatever I can to help you save the girl."

"I don't take chances." Jake moved toward the rim of the box canyon, crouching, and finally dropping to his stomach and crawling the last few yards. His hunch about this place had been right—someone had set up camp down below, with a tent tucked into the cover of trees, a campfire ring and various supplies scattered about. As he scanned the area a slight figure emerged from the trees—Sophie. She was bound hand and foot, her head down, shoulders slumped. The sight rattled Jake—it took all he had in him to push aside the rage and fear that threatened to crowd out everything else in his head. He had to keep it together if he was going to save her.

Another figure emerged from the woods behind Sophie. Carmen walked with her head up, her expression fierce, and Jake had to bite the inside of his cheek to keep back a roar of rage. He had expected to find Sophie here and had prepared himself for that. But seeing Carmen held prisoner touched something deep inside of him, a core need to protect the woman he loved, whatever the cost.

He hadn't let himself admit he loved her until that moment. He had been on his own since he was a teenager. He didn't need other people. He certainly didn't need a woman. Yet right now, at the very core of his being, he needed Carmen. He needed her faith and trust in him, and he needed to be the man he saw reflected in her eyes when she looked at him with love.

He crawled back from the edge of the canyon, then stood and raced back to Werner. When he pulled out his knife, the German shrank back, wide-eyed, but Jake only cut the plastic cuffs, then pulled out the keys to his truck and pressed them into Werner's hands. "Do you remember where I parked?" he asked. "Can you get back there?"

"Yes, yes."

"Drive to Ranger headquarters. Let them know where I am."

"You have found him?"

"Yes. Can you give the Rangers directions to this place?"

"Yes. What are you going to do?"

"I'm going to keep an eye on him until you bring help." He put a hand on Werner's shoulder. "I'm trusting you on this. If you steal my truck and drive away without getting help, I'll spend the rest of my life hunting you down."

Werner nodded again. "I will bring help, I promise."

"I'm counting on it." He clapped the older man on the back. "Now go."

As soon as Werner was out of sight, Jake moved back to the canyon rim. Stealthily, he dropped down, moving from the cover of rocks to trees to shrubs, until he was only a dozen yards above the trio in the camp and could hear them clearly. Then he settled in to wait for either the Rangers or the Russian to make a move.

CARMEN WORKED TO keep her expression calm and impassive as the Russian talked on and on about first one subject, then another. She had met his type before—give him a captive audience, and he would recite the history of the wrongs that had been done him. Since she was Native American, a member of another oppressed group, she was supposed to sympathize.

Beside Carmen, Sophie sat very still. Carmen worried the girl was in shock. She hadn't said a word since they had returned from a short trek into the woods, where Petrovsky had allowed them to relieve themselves, Carmen standing as a shield for the girl. When the Russian turned his back for a moment, Carmen tried to catch Sophie's eye. She gave her a look that was meant to be encouraging, but the girl didn't respond.

"The people in the United States still see Russia as their enemy," Petrovsky said, turning back to them. "They look at every Russian as if he is a criminal, and they don't want to do business with me.

"Your people—" he pointed to Carmen "—they are different. They are outsiders, too. I think we could do business. I have experience they could use. I know how to get back at the Americans who have taken advantage of us for too long."

Carmen could have pointed out that the Southern Ute were not a bunch of naïve savages but successful businessmen and -women in their own right. They didn't need to take revenge on anyone. But arguing with the Russian wouldn't gain anything. She needed to stay in his good graces and watch for the opportunity to flee with the girl.

"My stomach hurts."

The sudden outburst from Sophie startled Carmen and cut off Petrovsky in mid-sentence. "What?" he barked at her.

"My stomach hurts," she said. "I have to go to the bathroom again."

"No!"

"Please!" She doubled over, hugging her stomach. "I have to."

"Do you think I am stupid?" Petrovsky asked. "If I let you go off in the woods again, you will try to run away."

"No, I won't," Sophie said. "I promise."

Carmen studied the girl. Something in her tone didn't ring true. Petrovsky was probably picking up on that. She was a terrified fourteen-year-old— Sophie gave her props for trying. But what had prompted her sudden acting job?

A flicker of movement in the bushes over Petrovksy's shoulder caught her attention. Someone was up there. No wonder Sophie had felt the need to cause a distraction. "I think she's telling the truth," Carmen said. "You'd better let her go."

"Please let me go!" Sophie wailed.

Carmen squeezed her hand, both to signal that she should tone down the overacting and to distract her from looking behind Petrovsky, where Jake was visible through the trees, moving stealthily toward them. But he still had a ten-yard gap of open space to cover to reach them.

"What are you looking at back there?" the Russian demanded. He drew his pistol and whirled, just as Jake stood and aimed his own weapon.

Carmen pulled Sophie down on the ground beside her, out of the range of fire. She heard a barrage of shots—maybe three or four—and the grunt of someone who had been hit. "Jake!" Sophie cried.

Carmen looked over her shoulder in time to see Petrovsky take aim at a large tree Jake must be using for cover. The Russian was hurt, blood running from his left shoulder, but the hand holding the weapon was steady. Sophie tried to break free of Carmen's grip. "We have to help Jake," she sobbed.

Petrovsky glanced back at them. When his eyes met Carmen's, she felt the cold of them clear to her heart. She pulled Sophie behind her and started backing toward the cover of the trees, even as the Russian swung around and aimed at her.

The shot went wild, the report of the bullet merging with the sound of the shot that brought him to his knees. He toppled over, dead from the bullet Jake had fired. Jake emerged from behind a boulder, the smoking weapon still in his hand. Carmen tried to walk toward him, a sobbing Sophie clinging to her, but her legs didn't want to work. She could only stand in place while he came to her, and the three of them embraced.

"I was going to wait for help," he said into her hair, between kissing it and stroking her shoulder. "But I couldn't be sure anyone would come, and I was too afraid to waste any more time."

"I knew you'd come." Sophie looked up at him, tears still streaming down her face.

"I wouldn't leave you." He wiped her tears away with his thumbs. "I won't leave you ever again."

She nodded and buried her face against his chest. He shifted his gaze to Carmen. "I won't leave you, either," he said. "If you're willing to let me stay."

"Just try to get away, Soldier Boy," she said and kissed him, the kind of kiss that said more than words and promised a lifetime of such kisses.

Epilogue

"Maybe I should have brought a gift or something." Jake tugged at the collar of his white Western shirt and loosened the turquoise and silver slide on his string tie. "A bottle of wine, or maybe some flowers?"

"There's no need for that." Carmen reached over from the passenger seat of her SUV and took his hand and squeezed it. "This is just a family dinner, nothing formal."

"A tribe is a kind of family, isn't it?" Phoenix spoke from the back seat. Carmen half turned to address the older woman. She had more color in her cheeks now, since she had completed the interferon treatments for her hepatitis C. She had put on a little weight and definitely had more energy. With proper care, she could remain in remission for years, possibly forever.

"A tribe is a real family," Carmen said. "One where people are related to each other by both blood and tradition."

"Are there any girls my age there?" Sophie asked. "Cousins or something?"

"I have a couple of cousins who have kids close to your age," Carmen said. "Girls and boys."

Sophie smiled shyly and smoothed the sides of her hair, which she had had cut last week into a fashionable, spiky bob. That and her new clothes made her look like any other teen girl, something Carmen knew delighted her almost as much as it worried Jake.

"Is Captain Tomato going to be there?" Jake asked.

"Chief Tonaho will not be there," Carmen said. "But, even if he is, I expect you to act like a gentleman."

"I'm getting better at controlling my temper," he said. "But you can't expect me to keep quiet if anyone says anything about him being your family's first choice for you."

"I do expect it," she said. "After all, you're my first choice, and that's all that matters."

Still holding Carmen's hand, he rubbed a finger over the large chunk of polished turquoise set in a wide silver band that she had selected instead of a diamond for her engagement ring. "Yeah, I guess you're right," he said.

"Will we get to see the place where you're going to have the wedding?" Sophie asked.

"Of course," Carmen said. "After dinner, we'll walk up there. You can see most of my family's ranch from there. I'll show you exactly where you'll stand during the ceremony."

"I can't wait," Sophie said. "Don't you wish you could get married today?"

"There's a lot to do to get ready for a wedding," Phoenix said. "The next two months will fly by."

"The main thing I'm waiting for is all the paper work to go through for my transfer to the Grand Junction field office," Jake said. "Ron Clark promised me it would be ready next week."

"You don't think anything will happen to hold it up, do you?" Phoenix asked.

"No. Clark is only too happy to get rid of me after he spent months—and a lot of resources—making a case against Werner Altbusser and ended up with nothing to show for it. With Petrovsky dead, his bosses didn't even think they had enough to go after the international organization and, by the time they got back to Werner, he had gotten rid of any of the cactus he'd collected on that last trip and was safely back in Germany, lawyered up and declaring his innocence."

"I hate that you worked so hard and have nothing to show for it," Phoenix said.

"Oh, I wouldn't say that." Jake slowed for the turn into the Southern Ute Reservation, and his eyes met Carmen's. "I'd say I got a lot out of this case. More than I'd ever bargained for."

She reached over and clasped his hand again. "I guess we both came out winners in this case," she said. All those years she had been so focused on proving herself, yet with Jake she didn't have to prove anything. She only had to love him, and be loved in return.

* * * * *

Look for the next book in Cindi Myers's THE RANGER BRIGADE: FAMILY SECRETS *mini-series,* MISSING IN BLUE MESA, *available next month.*

And don't miss the previous titles in THE RANGER BRIGADE: FAMILY SECRETS *series:*
MURDER IN BLACK CANYON
UNDERCOVER HUSBAND
MANHUNT ON MYSTIC MESA

Available now from Harlequin Intrigue!

SPECIAL EXCERPT FROM

FBI Agents Macey Night and Bowen Murphy
are on the hunt for a vigilante killer, but will the
dark attraction that burns between them
jeopardize their mission...and their lives?

Read on for a sneak preview of
INTO THE NIGHT,
the next book in the KILLER INSTINCT series
from New York Times *bestselling author*
Cynthia Eden.

THE LIGHT WAS in her eyes, blinding her. Macey Night couldn't see past that too-bright light. She was strapped onto the operating-room table, but it wasn't the straps that held her immobile.

He'd drugged her.

"I could stare into your eyes forever." His rumbling voice came from behind the light. "So unusual, but then, you realize just how special you are, right, *Dr. Night*?"

She couldn't talk. He'd gagged her. They were in the basement of the hospital, in a wing that hadn't been used for years. Or at least, she'd thought it hadn't been used. She'd been wrong. About so many things.

"Red hair is always rare, but to find a redhead with heterochromia…it's like I hit the jackpot."

A tear leaked from her eye.

"Don't worry. I've made sure that you will feel everything that happens to you. I just—well, the drugs were to make sure that you wouldn't fight back. That's all. Not to impair the experience for you. Fighting back just ruins everything. I know what I'm talking about, believe me." He sighed. "I had a few patients early on—they were special like you. Well, not *quite* like you, but I think you get the idea. They fought and things got messy."

A whimper sounded behind her gag because he'd just taken his scalpel and cut her on the left arm, a long, slow slice from her inner wrist all the way up to her elbow.

"How was that?" he asked her. His voice was low, deep.

Nausea rolled in her stomach. Nausea from fear, from the drugs, from the absolute horror of realizing she'd been working with a monster and she hadn't even realized it. Day in and day out, he'd been at her side. She'd even thought about dating him. Thought about having *sex* with him. After all, Daniel Haddox was the most respected doctor at the hospital. At thirty-five, he'd already made a name for himself. He was *the* best surgeon at Hartford General Hospital, everyone said so.

He was also, apparently, a sadistic serial killer.

And she was his current victim.

All because I have two different-colored eyes. Two fucking different colors.

"I'll start slowly, just so you know what's going to happen." He'd moved around the table, going to her right side now. "I keep my slices light at first. I like to see how the patient reacts to the pain stimulus."

I'm not a patient! Nothing is wrong with me! Stop! Stop!

But he'd sliced her again. A mirror image of the wound he'd given her before, a slice on her right arm that began at her inner wrist and slid all the way up to her elbow.

"Later, the slices will get deeper. I have a gift with the scalpel, haven't you heard?" He laughed—it was a laugh that she knew too many women had found arousing. Dr. Haddox was attractive, with black hair and gleaming blue eyes. He had perfect white teeth, and the kind of easy, good-looking features that only aged well.

Doesn't matter what he looks like on the outside. He's a monster.

"Every time I work on a patient, I wonder…what is it like without the anesthesia?"

Sick freak.

"But not just any patient works for me. I need the special ones." He moved toward her face and she knew he was going to slice her again. He lifted the scalpel and pressed it to her cheek.

The fingers on her right hand jerked.

Wait—did I do that? Had her hand jerked just because of some reflex or were the drugs wearing off? He'd drugged her when she'd first walked into the basement with him. Then he'd undressed her, put her on the operating table and strapped her down. But before he could touch her any more, he'd been called away. The guy had gotten a text and rushed off—to surgery. To save a patient. She wasn't even sure how long he'd been gone. She'd been trapped on that operating table, staring up at the bright light the whole time he'd been gone. In her mind, she'd been screaming again and again for help that never came.

"You and I are going to have so much fun, and those beautiful eyes of yours will show me everything that you feel." He paused. "I'll be taking those eyes before I'm done."

Her right hand moved again. *She'd* made it move. The drugs he'd given her were wearing off. *His* mistake. She often responded in unusual ways to medicine. Hell, that was one of the reasons she'd gone into medicine in the first place. When she was six, she'd almost died after taking an over-the-counter children's pain medication. Her body processed medicines differently. She'd wanted to know why. Wanted to know how to predict who would have adverse reactions after she'd gone into cardiac arrest from a simple aspirin.

It's not just my eyes that are different. I'm different.

But her mother…her mother had been the main reason for her drive to enter the field of medicine. Macey had been forced to watch—helplessly—as cancer destroyed her beautiful mother. She'd wanted to make a change after her mother's death. She'd wanted to help people.

I never wanted to die like this!

But now she could move her left hand. Daniel

wasn't paying any attention to her fingers, though. He was holding that scalpel right beneath her eye and staring down at her. She couldn't see his face. He was just a blur of dots—courtesy of that bright light.

She twisted her right hand and caught the edge of the strap. She began to slide her hand loose.

"The eyes will be last," he told her as if he'd just come to some major decision. "I've got to explore every inch of you to see why you're different. It's for the good of science. It's *always* for the good. For the betterment of mankind, a few have to suffer." He made a faint *hmm* sound. "Though I wonder about you...about us. With your mind...maybe...maybe we could have worked together."

And maybe he was insane. No, there wasn't any *maybe* about that. She'd gotten her right hand free, and her left was working diligently on the strap. Her legs were still secured, so she wasn't going to be able to just jump off the table. Macey wasn't even sure if her legs would hold her. The drug was still in her body, but it was fading fast.

"But you aren't like that, are you, Dr. Night?" Now his voice had turned hard. "I watched you. Followed you. Kept my gaze on you when you thought no one was looking."

She'd felt hunted for days, for weeks, but she'd tried to tell herself she was just being silly. She worked a lot, and the stress of the job had been making her imagine things. She was in her final few weeks of residency work, and everyone knew those hours were killer.

Only in her case, they literally were.

"You don't get that we can't always save every patient. Sometimes, the patients die and it is a learning experience for everyone."

Bullshit. He was just trying to justify his insanity.

"You see things in black-and-white. They're not like that, though. The world is full of gray." He moved the scalpel away from her cheek...only to slice into her shoulder. "And red. Lots and lots of red—"

She grabbed the scalpel from him. Because he wasn't expecting her attack, she ripped it right from his fingers, and then she shoved it into his chest as deep and as hard as she could.

Daniel staggered back. Macey shot up, then nearly fell off the table because her legs were still strapped and her body was shaking. She yanked at the straps, jerking frantically against them as she heard him moaning on the floor.

The straps gave way. She sprang off the table and immediately collapsed. She fell onto Daniel—and the weight of her body drove the scalpel even deeper into him.

"You...bitch..."

"You bastard," she whispered right back. Then she was heaving off him. Her blood was dripping from her wounds and she crawled to the door. He grabbed her ankle, but she kicked back, slamming her foot into his face, and Macey heard the satisfying crunch as she broke his nose.

He wasn't so perfect any longer.

"Macey!"

She yanked open the door. Her legs felt stronger. Or maybe adrenaline was just making her stronger. She ran out of the small room and down the hallway. He was going to come after her. She knew it. She needed help. She needed it *fast*. There were no security monitors on that hallway. No cameras to watch her. No help for her.

Her breath heaved out and her blood splattered onto the floor. She didn't look back, too terrified that she'd see Daniel closing in on her. The elevator was up ahead. She hit the button, smearing it with her blood. She waited and waited and—

Ding. The doors slid open. She fell inside and whipped around.

Daniel was coming after her. He still had the scalpel in his chest. *Because he's a freaking doctor. He knows that if he pulls it out, he's done. He'll have massive blood loss right away. But the longer that scalpel stays in...*

It gave him the chance to come for her.

His lips were twisted in a snarl as he lunged for the doors.

She slapped the button to close the elevator, again and again and again, and the doors *closed*.

Macey was shaking, crying, bleeding. But she'd

gotten away. The elevator began to move. Gentle instrumental music filled the air.

The doors opened again, spitting her out on the lobby level. She heard the din of voices, phones ringing and a baby crying somewhere in the distance. She walked out of the elevator, naked and bloody.

Silence. Everything just stopped as she staggered down the corridor.

"H-help me..."

A wide-eyed nurse rose from the check-in desk. "Dr. Night?"

Macey looked down at her bloody body. *"H-help me..."*

"I'VE FOUND HIM." Macey Night exhaled slowly as she faced her team at the FBI headquarters in Washington, DC. All eyes were on her, and she knew just how important this meeting was. She'd spent five years hunting, searching, never giving up, and now, finally... "I believe that I know the location of Daniel Haddox." She cleared her throat and let her gaze drift around the conference room table. "Daniel... the serial killer otherwise known as 'The Doctor' thanks to the media."

A low whistle came from her right—from FBI special agent Bowen Murphy. "I thought he was dead."

Macey had wanted him to be dead. "I never believed that he died from his injuries. That was just a story that circulated in the news. Daniel was the best surgeon I ever met. He knew how to survive."

"And how to vanish," said Samantha Dark. Samantha Dark was in charge of their team. The group had been her brainchild. Samantha had hand selected every member of their unit. The FBI didn't have official profilers—actually, "profiler" wasn't even a title that they used. Instead, Samantha and her team were called "behavioral analysis experts." But the people in that conference room were different from the BAU members who worked typical cases in the violent crimes division.

Each person in that small conference room—each person there—had an intimate connection to a serial killer.

Her gaze slid over her team members.

Samantha Dark…so fragile in appearance with her pale skin, dark hair and delicate build, but so strong inside. Samantha's lover had been a killer, but she had brought him down. She'd been the one to realize that personal connections to serial perpetrators weren't a weakness…they could be a strength.

Tucker Frost. The FBI agent's bright blue stare held Macey's. Tucker's brother had been a serial killer. The infamous Iceman who'd taken too many victims in New Orleans. His exploits were legendary—scary stories that children whispered late at night.

Her hands fisted as her gaze slid to the next

member of their team. Bowen Murphy. His blond hair was disheveled, and his dark gaze was intense as it rested upon her. Bowen had hunted down a serial killer, a man who the local authorities had sworn didn't exist. But Bowen had known the perp was out there. A civilian, he'd gone on the hunt and killed the monster in the shadows.

And then...then there was Macey herself. She'd worked side by side with a serial killer. She'd been his victim. She'd been the only "patient" to escape his care alive.

Now she'd found him. After five years of always looking over her shoulder and wondering if he'd come for her again. She'd. Found. Him. "You're right, Samantha," Macey acknowledged with a tilt of her head. "Daniel Haddox *did* know how to vanish." Her voice was quiet. Flat. "But I knew he wouldn't turn away from medicine. I knew he would have to return to his patients. He would *have* to pick up a scalpel again." But there had been so many places he could have gone. He could have easily stayed under the radar, opening up a clinic that dealt only in cash. One that didn't have any government oversight because it wasn't legitimate. One that catered to the poorest of communities.

Where he would have even greater control over his victims.

"I also knew that he wouldn't stop killing," Macey said. Once more, her gaze slid back to Bowen. She often found herself doing that—looking to Bowen.

She wasn't even sure why, not really. They'd been partners on a few cases, but...

His gaze held hers. Bowen looked angry. That was odd. Bowen usually controlled his emotions so well. It was often hard to figure out just what the guy was truly thinking. He would present a relaxed, casual front to the world, but beneath the surface, he could be boiling with intensity.

"Why didn't you tell me that you were hunting him?" Bowen's words were rough, rumbling. He had a deep voice, strong, and she sucked in a breath as she realized that his anger was fully directed at *her*.

"The Doctor isn't an active case for our group," Macey said. They had more than enough current crimes to keep them busy. "We have other killers that we have been hunting and I didn't want to distract from—"

"Bullshit." His voice had turned into a rasp. "You forgot you were on a team, Macey. What impacts you impacts us all."

She licked her lips. He was right. Her news *did* impact them all. "That's why I called this meeting. Why I am talking to you all now." Even though her instincts had screamed for her to act. For her to race up to the small town of Hiddlewood, North Carolina, and confront the man she believed to be Daniel Haddox. But... "I want backup on this case." Because the dark truth was that Macey didn't trust herself to face Daniel alone.

Samantha's fingers tapped on the table. "How can you be so sure you've found him?"

Macey fumbled a bit and hit her laptop. Immediately, her files projected onto the screen to the right. "This victim was discovered twenty-four hours ago." Her words came a little too fast, so she sucked in another breath, trying to slow herself down. "A victim who is currently in the Hiddlewood ME's office. The autopsy hasn't even begun, but the medical examiner was struck by what she felt was a ritualistic pattern on the victim." She licked her lips. "Look at the victim's arms. The slices, from wrist to elbow. The Doctor always made those marks first on his victims. Those are his test wounds. He makes them to be sure his victims can feel the pain of their injuries, but still not fight him."

Silence. Macey clasped her hands together. "We got lucky on this one because we have a medical examiner who pays close attention to detail—and who seems very familiar with the work of Daniel Haddox. Dr. Sofia Lopez sent those files to the FBI, and I've got… I've got a friend here who knows what I've been looking for in terms of victim pathology." When she'd seen those wounds, Macey had known she'd found the bastard who'd tormented her. "I think the man who killed this victim is Daniel Haddox, and I think we need to get a team up to Hiddlewood right away."

Tucker leaned forward, narrowing his eyes as he stared at the screen. "You think this perp will kill again? You're so sure we're not dealing with some copycat who just heard about Daniel Haddox's crimes and thought he could imitate the murders?" Tucker pressed.

No, she wasn't sure. How could she be? "I think we need to get up there." Her hands twisted in front of her. She wasn't supposed to let cases get personal, Macey knew that, but…how could this case *not* be personal? Haddox had marked her, literally. He'd changed her whole life. She'd left medicine. She'd joined the FBI. She'd hunted killers because…

Because deep down, I'm always hunting him. The one who got away. The one I have to stop.

Samantha stared at her in silence for a moment. A far-too-long moment. Macey realized she was holding her breath. And then—

"Get on a plane and get up there," Samantha directed curtly. Then she pointed to Bowen. "You, too, Bowen. I want you and Macey working together on this one. Get up there, take a look at the crime scene, and…" Her gaze cut back to Macey. "You work with the ME. If Daniel Haddox really committed this homicide, then you'll know. You know his work better than anyone."

Because she still carried his "work" on her body. And in her mind. In the dark chambers that she fought so hard to keep closed.

But now I've found you, Daniel. You won't get away again.

Tucker rose and came around the table toward her as she fumbled with her laptop. "Macey…" His voice was pitched low so that only she could hear him. "Are you sure you want to be the one going after him? Believe me on this…sometimes confronting the demons from your past doesn't free you. It just pulls you deeper into the darkness."

Her hands stilled on her laptop. She looked into Tucker's eyes and saw the sympathy that filled his stare. If anyone would know about darkness, it would be Tucker. She lifted her chin, hoping she looked confident. "I want to put this particular darkness in a cell and make sure he *never* gets out."

He nodded, but the heaviness never left his expression. "If you and Bowen hit trouble, call in the rest of the team, got it? We always watch out for each other."

Yes, they did.

She put her laptop into her bag. Tucker filed out of the room, but Samantha lingered near the doorway. Bowen wasn't anywhere to be seen. Macey figured that he must have slipped away while she was talking to Tucker. Clutching her bag, she headed toward Samantha.

"How many victims do you think he's claimed?" Samantha's voice was quiet as she asked the question that haunted Macey.

Every single night…when she wondered where Daniel was…when she wondered if he had another patient trapped on his table. *How many?* "We know he killed five patients before he took me." They'd found their remains in that hospital, hidden behind a makeshift wall in the basement. Daniel had made his own crypt for those poor people. He'd killed them, and then he'd sealed them away.

"He's been missing for several years," Macey continued. Her heart drummed too fast in her chest.

"And serial killers don't just stop, not cold turkey." Samantha tilted her head as she studied Macey. "He might have experienced a cooling-off period, but he wouldn't have been able to give up committing the murders. He would have needed the rush that he got when he took a life."

How many victims? "I don't know how many," Macey whispered. And, because she trusted Samantha, because Samantha was more than just her boss—she was her friend—Macey said, "I'm afraid to find out."

Because every one of those victims would be on *her*. After all, Macey was the one who hadn't stopped him. She'd run away from him, so terrified, and when she'd fled, he'd escaped.

And lived to kill another day.

Samantha's hand rose and she squeezed Macey's shoulder. "You didn't hurt those people—*none* of those people."

"I ran away." She licked her lips.

"You survived. You were a victim then. That's what you were supposed to do—*survive*."

She wasn't a victim any longer. "I'm an FBI agent now."

"Yes." Samantha held her gaze. "And he won't get away again."

No, he damn well wouldn't.

After a quick planning talk with Samantha, Macey slipped into the hallway and hurried toward her small office. As always, their floor was busy, a hum of activity, and she could hear the rise and fall of voices in the background. She kept her head down and soon she was in her office, shutting that door behind her—

"I would have helped you."

Macey sucked in a sharp breath. Bowen stood next to the sole window in the small room, his gaze on the city below. His hands were clasped behind his back, and she could see the bulk of his weapon and holster beneath the suit jacket he wore.

She put her laptop down on the desk. "Samantha said we should be ready to fly in an hour. She's giving us the FBI's jet to use—"

He turned toward her. "Do you trust me, Mace?"

Mace. That was the nickname he'd adopted for her, and half the time, she wasn't even sure that he realized he was changing her name. But…it was softer when he said "Mace" and not "Macey." For some reason, she usually felt good when he used that nickname.

She didn't feel good right then. *Do you trust me?* Was that a trick question? She frowned at him. "You're my partner. I have to trust you." Or else they'd both be screwed. She was supposed to watch his back, and he was supposed to watch hers. It was pretty much the only way the FBI worked.

He crossed his arms over his chest as he considered her. "I have to ask… What will happen if you come face-to-face with Daniel Haddox?"

She stared up at him, but for a moment, she didn't see Bowen. She saw Daniel. Smiling. His eyes gleaming. And a scalpel in his hand. The scalpel was covered in her blood.

Don't miss
INTO THE NIGHT
available December 2017 wherever
HQN Books and ebooks are sold.

www.Harlequin.com

INTRIGUE

Available January 16, 2018

#1761 OUT OF THE DARKNESS
The Finnegan Connection • by Heather Graham
High school sweethearts Sarah Hampton and Tyler Grant had their romance torn apart by a massacre. But now that they have a second chance, the horrors of their past prove to be closer than they ever imagined.

#1762 LAWMAN FROM HER PAST
Blue River Ranch • by Delores Fossen
Deputy Cameron Doran thought he'd seen the last of his ex, Lauren Beckett. But when she shows up on his ranch after a home invasion and with a shocking story about his nephew, he's not about to turn his back on her.

#1763 SECURED BY THE SEAL
Red, White and Built • by Carol Ericson
Britt Jansen will do anything to find her sister—including going undercover in the Russian mob, where she teams up with navy SEAL sniper Alexei Ivanov. But can she trust her secret with a man whose eyes are set on stone-cold revenge?

#1764 RANGER DEFENDER
Texas Brothers of Company B • by Angi Morgan
Texas Ranger Slate Thompson may be the only person who believes what Vivian Watts has been saying all this time—that her brother is innocent. But can he face down his own when evidence begins to point to police corruption in the case?

#1765 MISSING IN BLUE MESA
The Ranger Brigade: Family Secrets • by Cindi Myers
Michelle Munson has infiltrated a cult in order to uncover the truth about her sister's death. But when her baby is kidnapped, she knows she's in over her head. Ranger Ethan Reynolds may be her last hope in the Colorado wilderness.

#1766 LOVING BABY
The Protectors of Riker County • by Tyler Anne Snell
Chief Deputy Suzy Simmons isn't impressed by millionaire James Callahan's killer body or bulletproof charm. But when he draws her into an investigation involving a missing baby, she wonders why the man who has everything has taken on the case.

Get 2 Free Books,
Plus 2 Free Gifts—
just for trying the Reader Service!

HARLEQUIN
INTRIGUE

Tyler watched as she walked into the parlor. Sarah.
Whom he hadn't seen in a decade. She hadn't changed
at all. Yet she had changed incredibly. There was nothing
of the child left to her. Her facial lines had sharpened
into beautiful detail. She had matured naturally and
beautifully; all the little soft edges of extreme youth had
fallen away to leave an elegantly cast blue-eyed beauty
there as if a picture had come into sharp focus. She was
wearing her hair at shoulder length; it had darkened a
little into a deep, sun-touched honey color.

He stood. She was staring at him in turn.

Seeing what kind of a difference the years had made.

"Hey," he said softly.

They were both awkward, to say the least. She started
to move forward quickly—the natural inclination to hug
someone you held dear and hadn't seen in a long time.

He did the same.

She stopped.

He stopped.

Then they both smiled and laughed, and she stepped forward into his arms.

Holding her again, he knew why nothing else had ever worked for him. He'd met so many women—many of them bright, beautiful and wonderful—yet nothing had ever become more than brief moments of enjoyment, of gentle caring. Never this…connection.

He had to remember she had only called on him because their friend had been killed, and he was the only one who could really understand just what it was like.

They drew apart. It felt as if the clean scent of her shampoo and the delicate, haunting allure of her fragrance lingered, a sweet and poignant memory all around him.

"You came," she said. "Thanks. I know this is crazy, but…Hannah. To have survived what happened that October, and then…have this happen. I understand you're some kind of law enforcement now."

"No. Private investigator. That's why I'm not so sure how I can really be of any help here."

"Private investigators get to—investigate, right?" Sarah asked.

When the horror of their past is resurrected, can Tyler keep Sarah safe from a killer set on finishing what he started?

OUT OF THE DARKNESS by New York Times *bestselling author Heather Graham.*

Available January 16, 2018 from Harlequin® Intrigue.

www.Harlequin.com

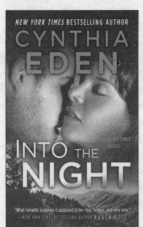

NEW YORK TIMES BESTSELLING AUTHOR

CYNTHIA EDEN

INTO THE NIGHT

"What romantic suspense is supposed to be—fast, furious, and very sexy."
—NEW YORK TIMES BESTSELLING AUTHOR KAREN ROSE

$7.99 U.S./$9.99 CAN.